THE AMISH FIREFIGHTER'S WIDOW

BOOK 8 EXPECTANT AMISH WIDOWS

SAMANTHA PRICE

Copyright © 2017 by Samantha Price

All rights reserved.

No part of this book may be reproduced in any form or by any electronic or mechanical means, including information storage and retrieval systems, without written permission from the author, except for the use of brief quotations in a book review.

Scripture quotations from The Authorized (King James) Version. Rights in the Authorized Version in the United Kingdom are vested in the Crown. Reproduced by permission of the Crown's patentee, Cambridge University Press.

This is a work of fiction. Any names or characters, businesses or places, events or incidents, are fictitious. Any resemblance to actual persons, living or dead, or actual events is purely coincidental.

CHAPTER 1

And we know that all things work together for good to them that love God, to them who are the called according to his purpose.

Romans 8:28

Katie leaned forward as far as her pregnant stomach would allow and traced two fingers over the name on her husband's headstone. It was six months ago that he'd died, and today she felt the need to visit his grave.

From her seated position on the blanket she'd brought with her, she looked around to make sure she was still alone. When Katie saw that she was, she wondered if it might be strange to speak to Luke aloud.

The two nights before Luke had died, Katie had been unable to sleep. She'd been restless and bothered as though she knew something was about to happen. Maybe God had given her a warning or sent a message to her heart that something was wrong. It was the Pattersons' barn that was burning and one of the *Englischer* firemen who lived closest to Luke and Katie, had collected Luke in his car.

It had been 'just another fire,' he'd told her before he'd kissed her goodbye in the dead of night.

She urged him to be careful. The last words she'd heard him utter before he closed the bedroom door were, 'I love you, Katie; go back to sleep.' Then he had come back and kissed her on her forehead before he raced from the room and down the stairs to jump in the other firefighter's car.

Luke had been an experienced firefighter, like his father before him. It was later found out that old Mr. Patterson had caused the fire by falling asleep next to a kerosene lamp in the barn. He'd woken to flames lapping the walls. Rather than run out of the barn, he had tried to put the fire out by banging burlap sacks against the heart of the flames. It wasn't long before the smoke overcame him.

After he had gotten the old man out, Luke ran back into the flames of the burning barn again and no one knew why. There was every possibility he had reason to believe that another person was still in the barn. No one had been able to answer the question of why Luke had gone back into the burning barn.

Katie had suspected that old Mr. Paterson had told Luke something that made him think there was somebody else in the fire; that's the only thing that made sense. But there were animals in the barn, so he might have died trying to free them.

Every time Katie thought about what happened in the fire that night, her stomach churned. She kept telling herself over and over that there was no use asking why he had to die, but she couldn't help it.

The inquiry into his death had produced no answer; all these months later she was still none the wiser as to why he went against protocol and rushed back into the fire.

A few hours after he died, it was just barely daylight, Luke's best friend, Mark, came to the door. Katie immediately knew something was wrong when she saw Mark, covered in black, standing at her door alongside the bishop. Instantly she knew Luke was dead. Neither man had to speak a word; the look on their faces said it all. She burst into tears, and then had to pull herself together to tell the boys what had happened.

The bishop had offered that he and his wife could look after the children for a few days, but Katie had wanted them close. Her children were all she had left and the closest thing to her husband. She didn't want to let them out of her sight.

Katie pulled her mind to the present and looked at the headstone. "Our baby is only weeks away, Luke."

It had taken Katie a while to adjust to the fact that her husband was not coming back and that she would be the sole parent of their two boys and the child that would soon be born. She'd often wondered if Luke would've been so determined to rush back into the barn if he'd known about the baby that she'd been carrying. She had suspected she might be pregnant, but she didn't want to tell Luke until she was further along since she'd had two 'false alarms' after their second child.

She continued, "Our *kinner* are good. The same as always—full of energy and full of fun. But I guess you probably know about that now; you can probably see everything from where you are."

The noise of a faraway buggy caused her to swing her head to the left. "It seems we're no longer alone and I don't like being here with other people about. I feel close to you here. It's not the real you lying in the ground. I know where you are." She pulled out her white handkerchief and blew her nose.

She tucked her handkerchief back into her sleeve, and kissed her fingers and then placed her fingers on the ground above his grave. "I will join you one day, but I have to stay until our *kinner* don't need me any longer. If *Gott* wills it I'll live long enough to see our *grosskinner*." Katie blinked rapidly and sniffed to hold back tears.

The other people had gone; she noticed when she looked around again. She'd stay then, and talk some more. "I still don't know whether we're having a boy or a girl although I always refer to the baby as a he. I wouldn't know what to do with a girl after having two boys. It would feel a little odd and I think we're having another boy. The boy's want a little *schweschder*. I suppose they've got each other to play with, so they could look after a girl. They've got each other to roughhouse with."

A small gray bird landed on the top of the headstone and looked at her.

"Hello, bird." She slowly put her finger out toward the bird. He cocked his head to one side and studied her for an instant before he flew away. "Mark is helping us all he can. He told me you asked him to look after us if anything happened to you. That made me think—did you know something was going to happen? I guess being a volunteer firefighter you were constantly putting your life in danger. I guess I knew that too, but it was something that I never believed would happen. I never thought you'd die. You'd been trained to avoid dangerous situations, so I don't know why you went back into that fire." Katie sat there in silence another half hour; she closed her eyes and imagined that Luke was sitting right next to her.

"I should go. Our *kinner* will be home from *schul* soon." Katie pushed herself up from the ground and then crouched back down to fold up the blanket she'd been sitting on. She took one last look at the grave. It didn't seem real that his body that was once so vibrant and full of life now lay lifeless, still and decaying. A bad dream is what it seemed like, but this was a dream from which she'd never wake.

Never had she even dreamed that she'd be left alone so young with three children. There hadn't been a firefighter killed in a fire for many years. Luke had never discussed with her what might happen if he died, but he had talked about it with Mark.

She took comfort in knowing Luke was with God and she would see him again. That knowledge gave her strength to go on.

Katie drove home in the buggy and when she pulled up, Marmalade, Mark's large orange dog, came bounding toward her. Wherever Marmalade was, Mark was never far away.

Katie looked up to see Mark and her boys outside the house.

Mark headed over to her. He was tall with a solid build, dark hair and eyes, and the tanned skin of a man who worked outdoors. Mark could've passed for Luke's brother.

"Hello, Mark."

"Hello, Katie."

The boys ran behind Mark to catch up to him while Marmalade insisted on getting a pat on his head from Katie.

"I'll look after the horse and buggy. Are you home for good or going out again?" Mark asked.

"Denke; I'm not going out again."

The boys hugged their mother, and James said, "You're late, *Mamm.* Where were you?"

"I was running some errands."

The boys walked to and from school and Katie was usually home when they got there, but with Nathan being nine and James eleven, they were old enough to look after themselves for a short time.

"You know I'll never be far." Katie realized it was Tuesday and Mark was there because he came for dinner every Tuesday and Thursday and had done so since Luke's death. She'd totally lost track of what day it was. Thankfully, she had some pork chops she could cook for dinner; she'd add some of her famous applesauce. The nights Mark came for dinner, Katie always made a special effort.

"You boys can help me unhitch the buggy while your *mudder* goes inside for a rest." He called Marmalade back from following Katie.

"Denke, Mark. I'll rest while I'm cooking dinner."

He laughed. "I suppose that's not much of a rest. The boys and I will help when we come in."

"Nee! That's girls' work," James said.

"I cook for myself, James. When you live alone you have to do it all. It doesn't hurt for a man to know how to do all those things."

"I guess so."

Katie smiled. "I've got the cooking under control. You boys do whatever you want and I'll find you when it's ready."

The boys were whispering to Mark, and laughing. She stopped walking to the house. "Mark, what are they trying to get you to do?"

"Build a tree house," Nathan said.

"That sounds like a fantastic idea," Katie said. "I would've loved to have one when I was a girl."

"It's for boys, *Mamm*, it's not for girls," James said.

Katie pulled a sad face. "Won't I be allowed?"

Mark waved his hands in the air. "Now wait a minute there is no tree house; don't encourage them, Katie."

Katie laughed knowing that if the boys were talking about a tree house, there was a very good chance that Mark was going to build them one. Not having children of his own, her children had become like his own.

The boys pleaded with the man they called Uncle Mark. "A tree house would be so much fun. You'd be allowed in," James said.

"If your *mudder* allows it I'll build you a tree house. Both of you will have to help me."

"*Jah* we will," they said in unison.

"Now where would it go?" Mark asked.

Katie cleared her throat.

"Oh, you haven't asked your *mamm*," Mark whispered to the boys.

"Can we have a tree house please, *Mamm?*" James asked.

"Please?" Nathan asked.

"Okay, you're allowed, but you have to help just like Uncle Mark said."

"We will," James said.

Both boys turned their backs on her and proceeded to help Mark with the horse and buggy, so Katie continued toward the house. Before she walked through the front door she called out, "Don't go too far. Dinner will be in about an hour and a half. And when you're choosing a tree, make sure it's on our land."

"Jah, Mamm."

"Jah, Mamm," James echoed his younger brother.

Katie enjoyed the nights Mark had dinner with them.

It was good to have another adult to talk with, rather than just her and the two boys all the time.

CHAPTER 2

And God shall wipe away all tears from their eyes; *and there shall be no more death, neither sorrow, nor crying, neither shall there be any more pain: for the former things are passed away.*
Revelation 21:4

As soon as Katie got into the house, she headed to the bathroom. Since the baby was getting bigger, her bathroom visits had become more frequent. Indoor plumbing was something she and Luke hadn't had as newlyweds, but when she'd become pregnant with James, their first child, Luke had gathered his friends and had built on a bathroom at the side of their house. Katie washed her hands and straightened herself up, pushing her loose strands of dark hair back beneath her prayer *kapp*.

"Now, it's peeling-potatoes time," she said to herself on her way to the kitchen.

∼

AFTER DINNER when the boys were doing their schoolwork in the living room, Mark helped Katie clean the kitchen and wash the dishes.

"Where were you today, Katie, when the boys came home from *schul?*"

Katie licked her lips. She knew he was inquiring because he was protective of her. She pushed her fingers into the warm sudsy dishwashing water. "It's been six months since the fire. I went to his grave."

"That explains why you've been looking so sad."

She shot her head up. "Have I? I hope I haven't been like that in front of the boys. Do you think the boys noticed anything?"

He smiled and shook his head. *"Nee.* Just relax; everything's fine."

"I don't want them to see me upset."

"You can't hide your feelings from them; they know when you do that. It's normal for you to feel sad that your husband has gone."

"I know, But I can't help the feeling that if I'm upset it will make them upset."

"Don't be troubled about so many things, Katie."

She looked into his face to see him smiling at her.

"Do I worry?"

"Yeah, you do. You often look upset and worried."

"Why have you never said anything up until now?"

"I didn't want to worry you any further. Worry you about looking worried."

"Thank you for being such a good friend and being with us through everything."

He chuckled and shrugged his shoulders.

"*Denke*, for being here for me and the boys. It helps to know that you're close by."

"Of course I would be here to help you. Luke was the closest friend I ever had and am ever likely to have."

"I know."

"Did you feel better for going to visit his grave?"

Katie nodded. "I did. I know you might think it's silly but..."

"You don't have to explain anything to me, Katie. As long as it makes you feel better that's all that matters. It doesn't matter if no one else understands it as long as it means something to you."

Katie smiled at him. It was as though she could do no wrong in his eyes. "That's the first time I've gone to his grave; the first time since the funeral. I know it's not really him there; I know he's with God, but I feel as if a piece of him is there in some way." Katie sighed. "Anyway, tell me about this tree house and the tree you found."

"We found a tree, a great tree. I can show you on

Thursday before dinner. It's too hard to tell you where it is."

"Okay, that would be good. Are you going to use the timber in the barn?"

"I could, and if there's nothing suitable I'll get bits and pieces from here and there."

"*Denke.* I wonder where they got the idea from."

"From me." He chuckled. "I was in the furniture store that my uncle and I supply and I saw some there. I thought the boys would like one. They seem to have a pretty clear idea in their heads how they'd like it." After he dried a few more dishes, he said, "Did James and Nathan tell you that they're hoping the baby is a girl?"

"Yes they have. I thought they would've wanted another *bruder*."

Mark shook his head. "Well they told me they wanted a *schweschder*."

"I suppose they have each other to play with so they don't need another boy to join in with their games. "

"I'm sure they'll be happy either way."

"We want a *schweschder*," James suddenly said, joining the conversation as he and his brother returned to the kitchen.

"You were talking like we weren't here," Nathan added.

Katie and Mark laughed.

"You won't have any choice, you know. We'll all have

to be happy with what ever *Gott* chooses for us," she said to her boys who both nodded.

"What's for dessert?" asked Nathan. "I'm still a little bit hungry."

"I made some apple crisp earlier. How does that sound?"

"Great!" said Nathan, as his brother and Mark smiled in agreement.

"I heard some news earlier today," Mark said when they were all settled back at the table. "Julie is coming back to the community."

"Julie Fuller?"

He nodded.

"That is a surprise."

"Is Julie your girlfriend, Uncle Mark?" Nathan asked.

"Nathan! You don't ask adults things like that!"

James laughed at what his young brother had said, covering his mouth with his hands.

Nathan turned to Mark "Sorry, Uncle Mark. I wasn't teasing you."

"That's alright. She was my girlfriend many years ago and we had talked about getting married, but then she left the community. I haven't heard from her since."

"So are you going to…?" James asked.

"James!"

"I'm sorry, *Mamm*. I didn't mean to be rude."

"Just mind your manners." Katie gave what she considered to be her best disapproving look at her oldest son and then looked at Nathan who was trying not to laugh. "Both of you mind your manners. You're each being just as naughty as the other. You can't speak to adults the way you talk with children your own age."

Mark turned to face Katie. "Just in case one, two or three of you were wondering, I'm not going anywhere. I'm staying right here. Someone needs to keep an eye on the three of you."

"Uncle Mark, if you ever get married will you still come and have dinner with us and still play with us?" Nathan asked.

"Of course I will. Now, no more talk about me getting married. If I were ever going to get married it would've happen a long time before now."

"Why don't you marry *Mamm?*" Nathan asked Mark.

James groaned. "Nathan, that's another embarrassing thing to say."

"Your *bruder* is right, you know better than saying things like that. A better conversation at the table would be to do with things that you did today—like how your schoolwork went. Maybe you could say what you learned at school. Don't say silly things."

"I didn't think it was silly." Nathan looked back down at his apple crisp.

"Your *mudder* and I are good friends, Nathan. Your *vadder* and I were friends—best friends. Just like you and James are."

"He's not my friend, he's only my *bruder,*" Nathan said.

The two boys looked at each other and screwed up their faces at each other.

"That's how it was for your *vadder* and me. Neither of us had any brothers, only sisters. We became friends because we were the same age and used to live next door to each other."

James rolled his eyes. "I know, I know. I've heard this story before."

"It's not a story, James. It's important for you two to remember as much about your *vadder* as you can. He would want you to grow up into honest hard-working men just like he was and just like your Uncle Mark is."

"*Jah, Mamm.*"

"*Jah, Mamm.*"

Katie wanted to hear more about Julie, but didn't want to talk any more about her in front of the boys. In her opinion Mark should speak with Julie if he hadn't already done so. He'd loved her once and Katie didn't want Mark to feel bound by his promise to Luke to look after her and the boys. It was a senseless waste for Mark not to carry on with his life as normal—when he could marry and have his own family.

When the boys had finished the last of their dessert, Katie said, "It's bedtime."

"So early?"

"*Jah.* Clean your teeth and go to bed."

"Can't we stay up and be with Uncle Mark for a few minutes?"

"Okay, but as long as you're ready for bed. Then you can stay up for fifteen more minutes."

"May we leave the table, *Mamm?*" James asked, as he'd been trained.

"You may," Katie said.

The two boys raced along the hallway into the bathroom.

"Ah, I wish I had their energy."

"It's only normal for you to feel tired isn't it?"

"*Jah* it is. I've been quite well, not like when I was having those two."

"That's good. I'll wash up these dishes. You sit there and rest."

"*Nee,* I can't watch you do that. I'll wash and you wipe."

"Okay."

When they were halfway through, the boys came back into the kitchen. "Tell us a story, please?" They both looked up at Mark.

Mark looked at her. "Is it okay if we go into the living room?"

"Of course."

Mark hung the dishtowel and headed off with the boys while Katie continued washing dishes.

He came back fifteen minutes later. "I've sent them to bed."

"Really? I didn't hear any fussing."

He raised his eyebrows. "They've gone to bed."

She giggled. "Okay I'll believe you."

He picked up the dishtowel and dried the dishes on the sink's drainboard.

When she'd put the last wet plate on the rack, she said. "Can you stay for a cup of hot tea?"

"I'd like that as long as I won't be in your way."

"Don't say things like that; you're never in my way. You're part of the *familye* to me—like an older *bruder*."

He placed the dry dishes in the cupboard. "While you're putting the pot on to boil, I'll go and see to the fire. It needed another log on it."

"Okay, *denke*." Once he was out of the kitchen, she wondered whether Mark had ever thought of her as more than a friend. She knew that there had been some talk in the community about them spending time together. Mark would certainly make anyone a fine husband, but she was pleased that he'd never put any unwelcome pressure on their relationship. It had been an awkward moment when Nathan had suggested to Mark to marry her.

"Okay, I've got the fire roaring; can I do anything in here?" Mark asked when he came back into the kitchen.

"When I put this hot water into the teapot you can carry the tray and set it down in the living room." She carried the teapot over to the sink and poured boiling water into it from the pot. She swished it around a couple of times and then set it down on the tray. "There you go."

Mark carried the tea tray into the living room and Katie followed close behind him.

She poured and handed him a cup after he'd put everything down on the table.

"*Denke,* Katie."

She sat down beside him and stared at the fire while she warmed her hands around her teacup. They sat for a while in silence, just looking at the roaring fire in the hearth.

"How has work been?" Katie eventually asked.

"It's been busy. The work has been pretty constant."

Mark worked for his uncle as a builder and had started to show the boys a few things about construction. Building the tree house together would surely give her boys some knowledge about carpentry, which wouldn't go to waste.

"That's *gut.*"

"Pamela said you hadn't been around to see her lately."

"I was planning to visit her tomorrow. Anyway, she can always come and see me." Pamela was one of Mark's sisters and had been Katie's best friend for many years.

He laughed. "I know, that's exactly what I said to her. She doesn't like to leave her *haus.*"

"I'm the opposite, I like to get out. So, you two were talking about me?"

"We were, but we were only saying really nice things."

"I hope so." She looked around for Marmalade.

"Where's that dog of yours? He's been dreadfully quiet."

"He fell asleep on your kitchen rug."

"It's a wonder he's not here by the fire like he normally is."

"I think our trek looking for the tree took its toll on him. He was running around sniffing animal trails and got himself totally worn out."

"Have you spoken to Julie since she's been back?"

"Nee. What we had was years ago. She'd be a changed person and I certainly am."

"She was the only woman you've been close to marrying, so there must have been something there."

"Ancient History." He took a gulp of tea. "Ow, that's hot! Now that you've brought the subject up I have had some things on my mind."

"Is there something you want to talk about with me?" Katie asked. "I hope I'm not prying into anything personal, but if you have a problem I'd like to help you with it." Katie thought he might talk more about Julie.

He rubbed his hands together. He took a deep breath and then squared his shoulders. "I'll be honest."

"Yes, that's always best." She closed her eyes for an instant, readying herself for him to say that he had decided to go and visit Julie.

"For the past few months I've been… well I've had this idea that I need to tell you about."

Katie frowned. "Does it have something to do with me?"

"It has everything to do with you."

"Tell me what it is."

He laughed. "I had hoped you'd guess so I wouldn't have to say."

"You're scaring me. What is it?"

"It's nothing worrying, Katie. I would like to marry you if you thought it was a good idea. I thought it might be an arrangement that would suit both of us. Soon you'll have three *kinner,* and I don't have a wife or a *familye* of my own."

"I don't know what to say." She stared at him, only too aware that he didn't speak of love. "I didn't suspect that you felt that way."

"It makes sense."

She stared at him again and wondered whether he was being practical or whether he was in love with her and was too nervous or shy to say it. How could she ask him which one it was? It didn't matter; it was too soon to think about another man. She had to be honest with him. "I would feel that I'm being unfaithful to Luke. It's too soon for me to even think of marrying again."

He nodded. "I understand. I just thought that the boys and you… well, it was just an idea."

"*Denke.* It was nice of you to offer. I'm grateful."

He nodded.

"Perhaps you should go and see how Julie is doing."

"I don't feel the need to marry someone. That's not the reason for asking you."

She poured more tea into his cup.

"I hope this won't ruin our friendship or make things awkward between us."

"*Nee*, it won't. Why would it?" Katie sipped on her tea, feeling that something *had* just changed between them. She'd always been able to relax when he was around, but now she'd always be wondering whether he saw her as a friend or as a potential marriage partner.

"I asked because I want to always look after the three of you, and the new baby—the four of you. I have no one to care for except your family and I already feel the responsibility and I was hoping we could make it official."

"Are we too much of a burden?"

"*Nee, nee* not at all. I never said you were a burden, but you are on my mind with every decision I make."

"I understand; there's no need to explain." Katie smiled at him but for the first time ever she wanted to be left alone so she could sort out the muddled questions that were firing off in her head. Maybe he had feelings for her and didn't know how to tell her, but then again, he could've felt a genuine sense of responsibility and that's why he'd proposed.

"I told the boys that if it was all right with you, we'd sort through the wood in the barn before dinner on Thursday and then we'd begin the work on it on Saturday."

"Saturday would be fine. I do have to see Maggie at eleven, though, on Saturday."

"The midwife?"

Katie nodded.

"I'll be here at ten and you can leave the boys here with me."

"That would work out well, *denke*." She laughed. "They don't like going anywhere where they can't run wild."

He smiled at her.

IT WAS an hour later that Mark left. After she'd placed the tea tray on the kitchen sink, she headed up the stairs to her bedroom. It had been a long and wearying day and she hadn't needed the upheaval of Mark proposing—not that it was a proper proposal, not a romantic one at least. Had it been a romantic one, it would've made her feel worse to turn him down, that was for sure and for certain.

Katie opened the door of Nathan and James' room to see that they were both sleeping soundly. She closed the door quietly and headed to her own room next to the boys' room.

Thinking about Mark again, something dawned on her. "I'm holding him back. He's spending so much time with me and the boys, that he's got no time to find a *fraa*."

There was only one thing for it. She'd have to let

him go. If she made him believe that the she and the boys didn't need him anymore he was more likely to make a life for himself rather than watching over them.

Giving the boys the go ahead on the tree house probably hadn't been the best idea, now that she was going to discourage Mark from spending so much time with them. As it was he came to dinner every Tuesday and every Thursday night, and called around to see them in between times.

Perhaps once the baby arrived she would have Mark come to dinner only one night a week. She could use the excuse that the baby was making her too tired for visitors. Even though Mark might see through that excuse at least that would give him more free time to find a wife of his own. Even with her baby weeks away from being born, Katie saw no need for a man in her life. Then it dawned on her. If Mark weren't at her house all the time to help her with everything and provide adult company, maybe she would've felt the need to marry again.

CHAPTER 3

If we confess our sins, he is faithful and just to forgive us our sins, and to cleanse us from all unrighteousness.
1 John 1:9

The next day, after Katie had taken the children to school, she stopped by Pamela's house.

Pamela ushered her into the living room. "Where have you been? I haven't seen you for a while. How's the baby doing?"

"Fine!"

"What's the matter? You look worried."

"There's nothing wrong; I'm just a little apprehensive with the baby due so soon."

"You still want me to be the birth helper, don't you?"

"*Jah*. You've been there for the births of the boys and I've been there for the birth of every one of yours, so I'm sure I don't want that to change." Katie smiled at her best friend.

After a few moments, Pamela asked casually, "Have you heard Julie's back in the community?"

"Julie Fisher?" Katie acted like she didn't know because Pamela liked to be the first to find things out.

"Yeah she's in Ohio and living with her Uncle Tom. I don't know if you know him—Tom Fisher?"

"*Nee*, I don't know him; has he been here—to our community?"

"I'm not certain about that, but you *do* know the Julie I'm talking about, don't you?" Pamela peered into her face.

"The girl Mark nearly married?"

"*Jah*, that's right."

"Have you talked to her since she's been back in the Ohio community?" Katie asked.

"*Nee*, I haven't. I've only heard from the The Morrisons that she's back."

"Surely she'll come back here where her *familye* is."

"Maybe." Pamela nodded. "I guess Mark hasn't mentioned anything to you about it; otherwise you would've known that she was back."

Katie took a mouthful of tea, hoping she wouldn't have to answer.

Pamela continued, "I haven't seen much of Mark lately; he's been keeping to himself a fair bit. Are you

Katie sighed. "I'm finally starting to see that, and that's something that'll have to change."

Pamela's eyes opened wide. "Why should things change?"

"Don't you see?" Katie stared at her friend hoping she wouldn't have to say what she meant.

"See what?"

"I'm holding your *bruder* back from finding love."

"I know it might be overwhelming for you with the *boppli* coming soon and that's why you probably can't think straight, but Mark is perfect for you. He's also perfect for the boys and I'm not saying that just because he's my *bruder*."

"The only man who can ever be my husband is no longer with us. I don't want to disrespect his memory by marrying again."

"That's what we're meant to do, marrying I mean. We're meant to have someone; that's just the way it is. Luke's not coming back, you're free to find someone, you don't have to stay alone."

"I know what you're saying, but I don't think you understand how I feel. I don't have to—or want to marry anybody."

"*Nee* of course you don't have to, but your life will be easier and better if you do. It would make me happy to see you married. I'm sorry, I don't mean to pressure you into anything." Pamela shook her head and smiled. "Forget I said anything."

With a grin on her face, Pamela added, "You answered quickly like you'd given it some thought."

Katie was not prepared to tell her friend that the only reason she had given it a lot of thought was that Mark had asked her to marry him. But the very way he'd asked showed her that he was approaching it from a practical point of view. Love had nothing to do with it. What she'd had with Luke was true love from the heart—the kind of love that comes once in a lifetime.

"Don't make a big deal of it or think something's going to happen between Mark and me, but the truth is I have thought about it and then decided against it. There, now you know."

Pamela shook her head. "Okay. I won't say any more." After a minute, Pamela said, "You're so stubborn, Katie. You don't know a good man when he's standing right before you.

Katie pressed her lips together and frowned.

to talk about their father. She never wanted them to forget him and how much he'd loved them. They spoke about him nearly every day.

"Each boy will be able to build his own *haus* by the time they're grown men. I'll see to that."

By his comment it was clear Mark was planning to be around for a long time.

"*Denke,* Mark. That will be a skill that will never go to waste no matter what they choose to do when they're older."

"I'm going to be a builder just like Uncle Mark, and fight fires like him too," James said.

Katie looked up at her two boys and wondered if they'd forgotten that their father was a firefighter and that was the very thing that killed him? It hadn't escaped her notice that James said a firefighter like 'Uncle Mark ' and not like his father. Was having Mark around causing the memory of their father to slip away?

Mark glanced at her, and then leaned in and said to the boys, "Don't forget your *vadder* was the very best firefighter around these parts. He risked his life to save a man. He was a fine man of *Gott.*"

"*Jah* we know that *Dat* was a firefighter just like you are. Also like *Dat's* friends. Nathan and I will fight fires too."'

"Maybe," Katie said. "You'll probably change your mind when you're older."

"I might, but I might not," James said.

Katie knew a change of subject was needed. "So what stage is the tree *haus* up to?"

Nathan answered, "Uncle Mark said before any building work starts we need to have a plan."

James continued, "Yeah, we must have a plan before we start, so we're gathering the wood and thinking about how we want it to be."

Mark added, "We've found enough wood. We've found the tree and we know exactly where to place the platform."

"*Jah* and now we have to figure out where we want the door and the windows," Nathan said.

"Doors and windows? This sounds like it's going to be a very fine tree *haus*. You're not going to move into the tree *haus* and leave me here all alone are you?"

"You won't be all alone, *Mamm*, you've got Uncle Mark," Nathan sniggered.

Katie frowned and looked across at Mark who remained stony-faced. Katie wondered if her boys had heard some of the community's gossip about the pair of them. Everything was pointing to her having to tell Mark not to come around so much. But then again, the baby wasn't far from being born, so what would happen if she needed his help after that? She couldn't tell him not to come around so much and then ask him back just because she needed a door fixed or there was something wrong with the buggy.

Katie knew she couldn't let what Nathan said pass

without reprimand. She frowned at him and he knew he was in trouble. "You shouldn't say things like that."

"Sorry, *Mamm,* and sorry Uncle Mark."

"*Jah*, it wasn't funny, Nathan," James told his younger brother.

Uncle Mark rubbed Nathan on the shoulder. "We all say silly things sometimes."

Nathan looked across the table at Mark. "Even you?"

"Sometimes. Just because I'm an adult doesn't mean that I don't make mistakes. I just don't make so many of them." He smiled and the boys chuckled.

"You'd better hurry up with that tree *haus* before the snow sets in," Katie said.

"It was cold out there today," James said.

"Well, you'll have to wear more clothes next time," Katie said. As Katie listened to her boys talk, she realized that this coming Christmas would be their first without Luke. Right there at the dinner table, she silently decided she'd had too many changes of late to tell Mark to stay away. He was her friend and she needed him around.

CHAPTER 5

*Therefore if any man be in Christ, he is a new creature:old things are passed away;
behold, all things are become new.*
2 Corinthians 5:17

~Weeks Later~

On Christmas morning, Katie woke to her baby's cries. Her little girl had been born three days ago. Katie was still in bed with the baby beside her. The baby had slept right next to her in the bed most of the night, as Katie had been too tired after the nightly feedings to put her back in the crib.

"Good morning, my *boppli.*" Her baby poked her tongue in and out. "Are you hungry again? You can't be.

I'm sure I've only just fed you. Maybe my milk will come in today and then you won't be so hungry."

Katie hurried downstairs while wrapping herself in her robe. The fire had to be started first thing to warm the small house. Once the first chore of the day was complete, she hurried back upstairs to give her baby another feeding. A little while later, she changed the baby's diaper, and just as she was placing all the dirty diapers into a bucket, she heard a buggy approaching the house.

Cradling the baby in her arms, she walked over to the window of her bedroom to see that it was Mark's buggy. She called out for the boys to let their Uncle Mark into the *haus*.

"Tell him I'll be down in five minutes."

"Okay, *Mamm*."

Christmas Day was the day that Katie had told Pamela to let people know she'd be ready for visitors. Katie knew that Mark would be excited to see the baby.

Katie's sister had offered to stay with her for the first few days, but since the birth had gone smoothly, and the boys were old enough to look after themselves, she didn't need to accept her sister's kind offer.

The baby fell asleep again just as Katie was wrapping her warmly.

"Don't you want to see your Uncle Mark?" she asked her baby quietly. "I'll still have to take you down so he can see you. I guess you can stay downstairs and that'll save me walking up the stairs again."

She placed her baby carefully on the bed so she could get dressed. First she pulled on her thick stockings, then her dress, and last she fixed her hair onto her head before placing on her prayer *kapp*. Once she'd tied her apron strings behind her back, she picked up the baby and headed downstairs.

Mark had been sitting on the couch waiting with the boys and when he saw her, he jumped up and waited at the foot of the stairs for her and the baby. "This is the young lady I've been waiting to see, " he said.

"Who, me or the *boppli?*" Katie jokingly asked.

"Both of you." He smiled at Katie and then gazed down at the baby. "Might I hold her?"

"Of course you can; you're her Uncle Mark." She passed the baby over and he cradled her in the crook of his elbow gazing down at her. "She's so beautiful, Katie. Just beautiful." He looked up at Katie. "And how are you? You look well."

"I'm feeling *wunderbaar.* The boys have been looking after me well."

He looked around. "Mind if I sit down?"

"Of course you can. You don't have to ever ask me that." She thought it funny that he'd asked because he'd already been on the couch waiting for her.

"You sit down too, *Mamm*. Nathan and I will make you and Uncle Mark a cup of hot tea," James said.

"You know how to do that?" Mark asked.

"*Mamm* showed us. If you show us how to do everything you know and she shows us how to do everything she does, we'll be able to do all the things that a man and a woman can do."

"That sounds like a mighty fine plan to me," Mark said exchanging a smile with Katie.

Once the boys were rattling around in the kitchen, Mark asked Katie, "Are you fine—really?"

"Everything went well and both of us are doing good. It was a bit startling to have a girl after two boys. It came as a surprise."

"*Jah* especially when you were convinced you were going to have another boy. I kept telling you she might be a girl."

"Did you?"

"*Jah* I did. Since you already had two boys the chances were in your favour of having a girl."

"I thought it was the other way around." Katie knew something had changed between them. Things had never been the same since he'd asked her to marry him. Now they were awkward with one another.

"I have presents in the buggy for the children and for you."

"I haven't even had time to think about that." She spoke without thinking because she'd had time to arrange presents for the boys. Realizing she hadn't told the complete truth, she added. "You never give me a present at Christmas time that's why I didn't think to get one for you."

"You don't have to give me one because I gave you one."

"It's not really like that. It's only the polite thing to do."

"We're friends. I don't think we have to worry about considering what's right and what's wrong, do you?"

She gave a little laugh to cover up her embarrassment over prattling on about gifts. "You've been so good to all of us. I should've been the one giving you a Christmas present, not you doing anything more for me."

"It's nothing much, just a token."

"You've made me feel very bad."

He chuckled. "I didn't mean to do that." He looked down at the baby. "Are they always this tiny?"

"She's about an average size; just over seven pounds."

"How long does she sleep?"

"She's taken to sleeping through the day and then she's awake during the night."

"That doesn't sound like a good arrangement."

"It's not! I'm trying to change that as quickly as I can. In time she'll adjust to knowing that night is for sleeping and days are for being awake."

The boys came back into the room.

"We're waiting for the pot to boil and we've got everything ready just like you showed us, *Mamm*."

"*Gut. Denke,* James."

Nathan stood beside Mark. "The *boppli* never sleeps. She cries all night."

"Right through the night?"

Nathan nodded. "She kept me awake all night last night."

"*Nee,* she didn't. I heard you snoring," James said.

"Well since the baby has been awake all night, maybe you boys can watch her while your mother gets some sleep later today."

"Okay," James said.

"We have a present for you, Uncle Mark," Nathan said.

"It's in the tree *haus,*" James added.

"Will you take me there to see what it is?" Mark asked.

The boys nodded with their faces beaming with delight.

"I know nothing about a present. When did you have time to get Uncle Mark a present?" Katie asked the boys.

"We made it. It's a secret that girls don't know about."

"What? Not even your *mudder?*"

"You're a girl!"

Mark laughed and then said to the boys, "And I have some presents for you two. They're in the buggy, and I'll fetch them after your *mudder* and I have that tea you're making." He looked down at the baby and then back up at Katie. "What have you called her? Have you named her yet?"

"Her name's Lillie. I wanted to give her a name starting with L for Luke."

"And *Mamm* said *Dat's* favorite flowers were lilies," James said.

"That's a beautiful name for a beautiful girl," Mark said.

"James, isn't the water boiling yet?" Katie asked.

James tugged on his younger brother's sleeve. "Come and help me make the tea. The boys hurried to the kitchen.

"Remember what I told you about that hot water?"

"I know, *Mamm*, I only half-filled it and Nathan is not to touch it," James called back.

"Very *gut!*" Katie shook her head.

"Are they excited about having a *schweschder?*"

"They were for the first day and then after that they complained that all she does is eat, sleep and produce too many dirty diapers. And cry at night."

Mark laughed. "Luke would've loved to see his little girl."

"He will see her one day." Katie appreciated that Mark felt comfortable enough to talk about Luke. Everybody else was too scared to mention Luke around her: she had noticed that.

. . .

WHEN THEY HAD FINISHED their tea, Mark handed Lillie back to Katie and then took the boys outside to give them their Christmas presents.

After she heard the boys squeal, Katie raised herself slightly from the couch to look out the window. The boys were riding around on bicycles.

She shook her head, and muttered to herself, "He shouldn't have spent so much money." The boys had been asking for bikes, but she'd been too worried about money to buy them. With the new baby, and without Luke's income, she had to be careful with money. She hoped that they hadn't given their Uncle Mark hints that they wanted bikes. She heard the front door open and close. It was Mark walking into the house by himself.

"You got them bikes?"

"I did."

"You shouldn't have spent so much money."

"It wasn't much." Mark placed a package on the table in front of her. "This is for you. I'll take Lillie so you can open it."

"*Denke.* You shouldn't have."

He gave a chuckle. "I didn't get anything for Lillie; I had no idea what people give newborns and I know she's got enough clothes. Pamela told me Lillie had more than enough."

She smiled at him and pulled on the red ribbon that was holding the glossy white paper. Inside the wrapping was a white paper box.

"Open it," he said.

Inside the box was a white china tea-set that was decorated with tiny red rosebuds.

"It's so beautiful." She looked up at him. "I think this is the nicest thing anybody's ever given me."

He smiled, looking pleased with himself. "Are you expecting visitors today?"

"I've got my sisters and their families coming to visit. They're bringing the Christmas meal with them, which I'm guessing is turkey and roasted vegetables. Will you join us?"

He shook his head. "I'm due at Pamela's *haus* shortly. I figure that I've got just enough time to make sure the boys know all the road rules and we can visit the tree *haus* and see how it fared in the snow we had a couple of days ago. And I can see my gift."

"I don't want them to ride on any busy roads."

"They won't be; just driving around these parts."

"Maybe when *schul* starts up again they might be able to ride to and from."

"I'm sure they'd like that; many children do that."

"Mark, something has been bothering me for some time."

Mark's soft brown eyes widened. "What is it? You must tell me. You need to tell me about all the difficulties you have."

"It's a hard thing to talk about, but I must say what's on my mind. You see, you spending all this time helping me and the boys, it's great for us, but I don't think it's good for you. I think it's holding you back."

He leaned slightly farther into the couch. "How could something like that possibly be holding me back—and holding me back from what?"

"Holding you back from finding a *fraa* and having a *familye* of your own."

He leaned forward and slowly nodded. "I've made my thoughts on the matter no secret to you."

"I can't marry again, Mark, I just can't."

He nodded. "I understand. I know that."

"Do you understand? Because I don't want there to be any problems between the two of us. The boys and I care about you very much. It would be wrong of me not to tell you what I've been thinking about you and your future."

"Now that you've brought the subject up—the bishop had a word with me and told me that there has been talk about us around the community."

"Rumors that we might marry?"

"Something along those lines."

"I've heard that." Katie played with the strings of her prayer *kapp*.

"Well, there's talk that I spend too much time here for a single man. He suggested that I be careful how much time I'm here."

Katie sighed.

"I know how the boys feel about me and I wasn't quite certain how you felt about me. I guess I was hoping for something more, but I didn't want to rush you. I thought in time…"

She shook her head. "Don't say more." Katie could see that the conversation wasn't going well and she couldn't let him think that there would ever be a chance for anything between them. He would just be forever waiting for something that would never happen, if she didn't tell him exactly how she felt.

It hadn't even been twelve months since Luke had died in the fire. Mark didn't need to waste all his time with them. She had to make him see that.

"Mark you're my favorite man in the world apart from my two boys. I think we need to listen to what the bishop said. You need to stop spending so much time with the boys and me so you can have a better life. It would be selfish of me if I didn't say anything to you. I love having you around and it's been good for the boys, but I can't be selfish. What I want for you is to find love and have a *familye*."

"That's something I want, but I too must be honest with my feelings; I was starting to think things would turn out differently." He looked directly into her eyes and her heart beat faster at what he might say next. He continued, "I believe I'm in love with you, Katie. And I couldn't love the boys any more if they were my own *kinner*—I'm certain of that."

For a fleeting moment she wondered 'what if?' What if she married Mark? Her children would have a father and she'd have a husband. Before long an image of Luke popped into her head. How would Luke feel about his best friend stepping in and taking his place? She looked back at Mark as he started to talk again.

"I will do as you suggest. I won't come here for dinner as I used to twice a week and I'll see you at the meetings instead."

"As hard as that is, that might be best."

"But if you need anything done around the *haus*, or if the boys need anything, please, let me know. Will you do that?"

Katie nodded. "I will."

He bounded to his feet. "I had better get the boys to the tree *haus* so we can get back in time for when your visitors arrive."

"*Jah* and before it snows again."

Mark smiled as he stood up. "That too." He looked down at the baby. "Do you mind if I hold her just one more time?"

"Sure." She offered Lillie up to him.

He cradled the tiny baby in his muscular arms. The sight of him holding Lillie so tenderly tugged at her heartstrings. When he looked up at her and smiled, she wondered if he knew her thoughts.

"I gave my word to Luke I'd look after you and your *familye* and that is a promise that I will keep, but from a distance. My desire to marry is not nearly as important as you think it is, but I'll respect your wishes."

"Everyone needs to have love in their lives."

"Doesn't that include you?"

"I've loved once and that's enough."

"Is it?"

She nodded. "It is."

"I understand."

Katie hoped that he did understand. She knew the boys would miss him, but she'd invite her sisters' families over more often and that included the boys' uncles and cousins. Surely that would help fill the gap that Mark's absence would leave in their lives.

CHAPTER 6

Repent ye therefore, and be converted, that your sins may be blotted out, when the times of refreshing shall come from the presence of the Lord;
Acts 3:19

Nearly a whole year had gone by and it was into November—almost time for the wedding. Katie had heard that Julie would be at the wedding the next day. Jerry Lapp and Carmine Fuller were to be married and Carmine was Julie's cousin. It was more than likely that Julie would be amongst the hundreds of guests at the wedding.

In the months that Mark had stayed away from Katie, he hadn't made any effort to find a wife. Katie knew that for certain because Mark's sister, Pamela, had told her so. Now, Katie had just pulled up at Pamela's house to find out if Mark and Julie had been communicating. Perhaps they'd talked on the phone or had exchanged letters. At any rate, Pamela always knew what was happening.

Katie had left the boys with one of her sisters and taken Lillie with her.

"Where is she?" Pamela came running out of the house and whipped Lillie out of the buggy. "Here you are," she said to Lillie.

Lillie giggled as she grabbed at Pamela's *kapp* strings.

"Don't I even get a 'hello'?" Katie asked.

Pamela spun around and giggled. "Hello, Katie. Come inside; it's freezing out here."

Katie put Lillie down on a rug with some toys in Pamela's living room. It didn't take long for the conversation to work its way around to Jerry and Carmine's wedding.

"You know, he wasn't her first choice," Pamela said regarding Jerry.

"*Nee*, I didn't know that."

Pamela nodded. "She was in love with Toby Hostetler."

"Really? I don't see them together at all. He seems too carefree for her."

"Now Toby's set to marry Jessica."

"Toby and Jessica?"

Pamela nodded again.

Katie pulled a face. "I don't know anything that's happening about the place anymore."

"Well, you have been busy lately with Lillie."

As casually as she could, Katie asked, "Do you know if Julie Fuller will be at Carmine's wedding since she and Carmine are cousins?"

"That's what I've heard; that Julie's coming, and that she might stay on."

Katie didn't like the sound of that. "Why would she? Julie hasn't been back here since she returned to the community more than a year ago."

Pamela stared at her.

"I mean, I'm just wondering."

"Sounds like you're a bit jealous, Katie."

"Who would I be jealous of? You mean Julie?"

"*Jah*, Julie because she once nearly married Mark."

Katie shrugged her shoulders. "I barely know her and I haven't seen her for years."

"You're worried that Mark and Julie will rekindle a romance."

"I am not! I hope he does marry her or someone else. He needs a *fraa*."

"He does. That's what I keep telling him."

"And what does he say?"

Pamela laughed. "I can't tell you that."

"Why not? I thought we were friends. You usually tell me everything."

"We are friends. You're my closest friend."

"Well, tell me, then," Katie insisted.

"Nee!" Pamela shook her head. "I can't tell you something that I had to pry out of him."

"So there is something and it might involve me and that's why you won't say."

Pamela frowned and leaned closer to Katie. "Why would it involve you?"

She'd gone too far. Pamela wouldn't know what had happened between Mark and her, and now she'd opened her big mouth. The other bad thing was that from Pamela's reaction, Mark had confided in her about someone else. Perhaps Mark had moved on and forgotten her.

"There's no reason. Don't mind me. I'm just concerned that he find someone and that's what I told him," Katie said.

"Gut! Maybe if people keep telling him the same thing he'll start listening."

"I hope so." Katie had gotten some information out of Pamela, but it wasn't the information she'd wanted to hear.

~

THE WEDDING of Jerry and Carmine was an early morning ceremony. Knowing that she would see Mark made Katie agitated. She wasn't looking forward to finding out how Mark would react to seeing Julie. There was something going on and Katie knew that from Pamela's strange response to her questions regarding Mark.

It was possible that Mark and Julie had been corresponding and perhaps this is where they would reunite—at Carmine's wedding.

"Come on, *Mamm*, you don't want to be late. Uncle Willis will be here any minute and you always say not to keep people waiting," Nathan called to her from the bottom of the stairs.

"I'm coming," she called back from her bedroom. She picked up Lillie, who shared her bedroom in their small two-bedroom home, and carried her down the stairs. Once she was at the bottom, she placed Lillie on her own two feet since she was starting to walk.

The boys each took one of Lillie's hands and lifted her in the air, taking her to the front door. Lillie squealed with delight.

The first few weddings that Katie had been to without Luke had been hard, but now she was more used to him not being with her. Nevertheless, she always shed a quiet tear when the couples were pronounced married.

When they arrived at Carmine's parents' house for the wedding, Katie was determined to watch both Mark and Julie closely. Katie grabbed Lillie's hand and headed for the back row where she would get a better view of everyone.

Julie came down the stairs right before Carmine. It appeared Julie was one of Carmine's attendants. No one had told Katie that. Surely that meant that Julie had already been to Lancaster County at least once or twice to help with the wedding preparations.

More people walking into the house caught her attention. Pamela walked through the door and waved to Katie. As soon as she waved back, Mark came through the door and thought she was waving at him. He waved back and gave her a huge smile.

Katie smiled at him and then quickly looked away. A minute later, she looked back at him just as he was about to sit down and saw that he had caught Julie's eye.

Julie smiled at Mark and Katie's stomach churned at the sight. There *was* an attraction between them. Something within her didn't want him to like Julie, but then again, it wouldn't be fair to hold onto him. She had to release him if she wasn't going to marry him.

When the wedding was over, the bride and groom, and all the attendants apart from Julie, walked outside. Julie waited, staring directly at Mark. Since everyone else was on their feet now and moving towards the door, Katie had no choice but to join the crowd.

Katie was one of the last people out of the house and she noticed that Mark was making his way to Julie.

The guests were to stay outside while the men exchanged the wooden benches for long tables for the food to be served. Ten minutes later, everyone was heading back into the house. The first thing Katie did was look around to find Mark and Julie. Then she saw them chatting in a corner of the room. Katie took a good look at Julie who didn't look a day older than she had many years ago before she'd left the community.

When Mark and Julie finished talking, Mark headed to talk with a group of people who were on the opposite side of the room. All Katie wanted to do was go home. Was she in love with Mark, or was it simply male attention that she missed?

CHAPTER 7

My little children, these things write I unto you, that ye sin not And if any man sin, we have an advocate with the Father, Jesus Christ the righteous:
1 John 2:1

Two weeks later, Mark came to the house just before the boys were due to come home from school. Lillie was having a nap, so Katie went out of the house and waited by the front door for him to tie up his horse.

"It's just like old times, " she called to him with a smile.

"It is, except for the purpose I'm here."

Had he come to tell her that he and Julie were

seeing each other—dating? She stepped back. "Come inside and I'll make us a cup of hot tea."

He rubbed his hands together. "Yeah that would be good. I need something to warm me up."

Once they were both seated at the kitchen table with their cups of tea, he began, "I've come to let you know that I'm going to Ohio for a couple of weeks. I didn't want you to hear any talk about why I'm going—or anything like that."

"Ohio?" Was he going to Ohio for Julie? She'd heard Julie had gone back to stay with her cousins in Ohio.

"It's got nothing to do with Julie if that's what you're thinking."

"I wasn't thinking anything of the kind."

"I'm doing a job there through to the end of January."

"What kind of a job?"

"I'm going to be training volunteers for the fire department."

Katie grimaced. She knew people had to fight fires, but she wished that Mark wasn't doing something so dangerous.

"I know you don't like talking about fire or anything to do with it, but it needs to be done. It's a way we can serve the community."

"I know. " She looked down at the palms of her hands under the table. "It's good of you to give your time like that and teach people what you do."

"If they're taught the right way they keep safe themselves. The other thing is that they need more people to volunteer."

"You're going to talk to the men in the community about volunteering?"

He nodded. "I am."

"*Denke* for coming to say goodbye yourself. I'm sure there will be a lot of rumors floating around. Has Julie gone back to Ohio? I'd heard that she had."

"*Jah*. She was only here for Carmine's wedding."

"I thought that when I didn't see her at the Sunday meeting the week after the wedding. Seems I'm the last to know a lot of things these days." She gave a little laugh. "Who will you be staying with?"

"That's the other thing I meant to tell you. I'll be staying with Julie's *bruder's* family."

Katie raised her eyebrows. "Julie has a *bruder* in Ohio? I never knew that. I thought all her *familye* were here except for an uncle and a couple cousins."

"Her youngest *bruder* went there two years ago to get married."

"I didn't know that. I don't know any of Julie's *familye* very well at all."

If Mark was staying at Julie brother's house he'd be seeing more of Julie.

"The boys still play in the tree *haus* they told me."

"Nearly every day of summer, but not so much in the cooler weather." She laughed. "They love it. They'll use it for many years to come."

"I'm glad." He drained the last of the tea in his cup. "I'll be on my way."

Katie bounded to her feet. "Don't go. Have another cup of hot tea."

He shook his head. "*Nee denke.* I just remembered there's something I need to do that I haven't done yet. It's urgent." With that, he rushed out the door without even waiting for Katie to see him out.

She sat there dumbfounded, wondering if she had said or done something to upset him.

∽

THE BOYS CAME HOME from school upset, and they were a little cranky when they heard that they'd missed seeing their Uncle Mark, but he had left them presents.

"He was in a hurry and said he'd forgotten to do something. He'll be away for a few weeks. He'll come and see us when he gets back. He's going to Ohio for some time; until the end of January."

"I'd rather him be here for Christmas, rather than having a present," Nathan said.

"Why doesn't he come around here anymore like he used to?" James pouted.

"Where is Ohio?" Nathan asked.

"A long distance away," Katie said.

"Why doesn't he come to the *haus* like he used to?" James repeated. "He used to be here nearly every day."

"He's a very busy man. He's got lots to do."

"Didn't he always have lots to do?" James asked.

"Why don't you to go out and play and I'll bake some cookies?"

James jaw dropped open. "Don't we have anything to eat now?"

Nathan grumbled, "Yeah I'm starving."

Normally Katie had food waiting for them after school, but her head was in a spin from Mark's visit. "I can heat up some of the soup that we're having for dinner."

"Will that be long?" Nathan asked.

"I'll put it on right now. And while it's heating up you can have bread and butter."

The boys sat at the table, spreading butter on the bread.

"I hope Uncle Mark comes to visit us as soon as he gets back." Nathan bit into a slice of bread.

James nodded. "*Jah!* The minute he gets back."

"That would be nice," Katie said. "James can you go up and check on Lillie? She should be awake by now."

"Okay, *Mamm*."

James walked Lillie downstairs and the three children sat and had something to eat. While they ate, Katie thought some more about Mark and realised that he hadn't brought Marmalade over the last few times he'd visited. Neither had he asked her to look after the dog, and in the past, she'd always looked after Marmalade whenever Mark had gone away for longer than a day. Things were so different now and the year apart from Mark had already been difficult, so she knew she wouldn't like him being so far away in Ohio.

"When you boys go out to play, make sure you wear your coats. It's cold out there."

"We will, *Mamm*."

"Can Lillie come and play with us?"

"*Nee*, she's still too young. You could play with her inside."

"We've decided to let her play in the tree *haus* when she's older," Nathan announced.

"That's very kind of you. But she'll have to be a lot older to get up the ladder."

When the boys went outside to play, Katie made cookies and couldn't get her mind off Mark.

It was only after dinner that night that James told her something that shocked her.

"I forgot to tell you that I invited people to dinner on Wednesday night."

"You did?" Katie looked at James with raised eyebrows; this was the first time he'd done anything of the kind.

"*Nee;* it was Tuesday night," Nathan corrected him.

"That's right, it's Tuesday night."

"You invited someone to dinner without asking me, James?"

Both boys nodded.

"You shouldn't do that. You should've asked me first."

"I'll know that for next time, *Mamm*," James said.

"Who did you invite?"

"Mr. Bontrager and his two boys."

"His two boys are about your ages aren't they?"

When James and Nathan sniggered and elbowed each other Katie knew they were trying to match her with Samuel Bontrager, a widower. "It's okay this time, but remember to ask next time before you invite someone. I could've had something else arranged."

"We didn't think you would have because Tuesday and Thursday nights are always the nights that Uncle Mark used to come here for dinner," Nathan said.

"And he hasn't been to dinner for a long, long time," James added.

"One thing you'll learn about in life is that everything is constantly changing. Nothing ever stays the same."

The boys nodded and stared at her with wide eyes.

"Take Lillie with you and go brush your teeth."

"*Jah, Mamm.*"

"*Jah, Mamm,*" Nathan echoed his older brother.

As soon as the boys and Lillie were out of the room, Katie sighed deeply. Samuel was a nice man, but he was well known for being desperate to get married again. Rumor had it that he'd already asked a couple of much younger women to marry him and naturally they had refused. Now her boys had put her in an awkward situation. Were the boys so desperate to have a father that they were taking it upon themselves to actively find her a husband?

At the next Sunday meeting, Katie knew she'd have to say something to Samuel about coming to dinner. Katie was embarrassed to face Samuel in case he thought she had put the boys up to asking him to dinner. It seemed some people in the community had been gossiping about her and Mark being interested in one another, so how would it look the moment Mark left town that she had Samuel to the house for dinner?

When the meeting was finished, Samuel walked right up to her.

"Hello, Samuel."

He smiled and gave her a nod. She didn't know him very well, but he had a reputation as being a decent man and a good father. His wife had died two years before Luke had died.

"Your boys have invited me and my boys to dinner." He laughed. "It was lovely of them, but I wanted to check with you first to make certain you were aware of the invitation."

She was relieved that he knew she hadn't asked the boys to invite him. "*Denke*. Nathan told me he'd invited you for Tuesday, and I'd intended to talk to you about it today and make sure you could come."

"I can certainly come. I'd be delighted to come for dinner," he said with a smile.

Looking around her, she was pleased they were alone and no one could hear their conversation. "There's just one thing I want to say."

"Jah, what is it?"

"I think my boys are looking for a new *vadder* and that's why they invited you for dinner."

His eyebrows flew up. "Do you think so?"

She nodded.

"Your boys get on with my two; I figured that's why James invited us to dinner."

"I know, but they were attached to Mark and now he's gone to Ohio for a while. I think they miss having a man about the place."

"Do you want me not to come?"

"Nee, nee. I'd love you and the boys to come for dinner. But I must say that I'm not looking for a husband."

He laughed. "I'll remember that."

"Oh, I didn't mean that..."

He shook his head. "You don't need to say anything. I understand what you mean."

"You do?"

He nodded.

"Denke."

He laughed again. "It's good to know your boys think I'm worthy enough for something like that."

Katie smiled, pleased with herself for telling him

her situation upfront. He was easy to talk with and she thought they might become friends.

"It's good to be honest about things," he said.

She gave a little laugh, glad that she hadn't hurt his feelings.

"The first year after my *fraa* died I was lonely, but now I've grown used to my life without her. I'm quite comfortable now, but I guess you've heard I did make a fool of myself?"

"I think we've all made fools of ourselves at one time or another." She smiled at him now thinking of him in a totally different way. He was gracious, kind and honest.

Pamela came up to them and took hold of Katie's arm. "Hello, Samuel, will you excuse us?" she said.

"Yes, of course." Samuel took a step back.

"I thought I'd rescue you before he asked you to marry him."

"Don't be like that; he's a nice man."

"I know he's a nice man, but he goes around asking everyone to marry him. You won't marry my *bruder* so you're not going to marry Samuel."

Katie stopped walking. "My you're bossy. Who made you in charge of my life?"

Pamela laughed. "I'm helping you."

Katie shook her head at her friend. "You know far too much about my life." Although she said it jokingly she really meant it. It wasn't nice how Pamela had pulled her away from Samuel.

"My *bruder* is a much better match for you than Samuel."

"I'm not looking for anyone at all."

"You'd do well to make sure you're not gonna change your mind soon because, don't forget, my *bruder's* in Ohio and so is Julie."

"Have you heard from him?" Katie asked.

"Nee."

When they'd finished talking, Pamela walked away. Katie wondered if a good way to get over Mark's absence was to make friends with Samuel, but then again, she didn't want to lead Samuel on either. If she and Samuel developed a close friendship there was always a risk that one of them would get hurt.

She'd have to tell the boys once more never to invite anyone for dinner without asking her first. At least she'd been honest with Samuel and he'd been honest with her.

CHAPTER 8

*If ye know these things,
happy are ye if ye do them.*
John 13:17

School had finished for the year and when the boys came home from playing with their neighbors on Tuesday afternoon, they were excited about having the Bontragers over for dinner. Katie had made a roast pork dinner with roasted vegetables and sauerkraut, and a pumpkin pie with fresh cream for dessert.

As soon as the boys heard the buggy at five thirty, they were out the door running to meet their friends.

Katie waited at the door for Samuel to tie his horse,

and when he'd finished he looked over and waved to her.

"Hello, Samuel." She smiled at him.

He walked toward her. "Hello, Katie."

"Come inside out of the cold."

"Gladly," he said before he walked through the door.

She showed him through to the living room. "Have a seat."

"Thank you." He looked around. "The *haus* is cozy."

She laughed. "That's a nice way to say tiny, but it was only meant to be a temporary *haus* for us. Would you like a cup of tea? I've got the pot boiled."

"I'd love one, *denke.*"

She headed to the kitchen, glad that the boys had initiated this friendship. It was nice to have a man over for dinner again.

She brought the tea out and placed it on the low table in front of the couch.

"Dinner smells amazing," Samuel said.

"That's good. I hope it tastes amazing too."

"I'm sure it will." He looked around again. "Where is your *dochder?*"

"Lillie's having her afternoon nap. She's sleeping a little later than usual."

"Ah, I remember the afternoon naps. Unfortunately, they grow out of that far too quickly. Enjoy it while you can."

Katie giggled. "It does give me a little bit of a rest." She poured a cup of tea and passed it to him.

"*Denke.* The boys certainly enjoy playing together."

"They do."

"Are you coping all right since Luke's been gone?"

"It's taken a while to adjust, but I'm getting better all the time. It's sad that my *dochder* will never know him."

"It would be." He nodded. "Do you get lonely?"

"My *kinner* keep me busy. I guess I've adjusted to life without him, and some things just can't be replaced."

"You mean some things and some people can't be replaced?"

She nodded. "That's right."

It seemed as though he was now resigned to the fact that he would never marry again just as she was.

Dinner had gone well, and there was never a moment when the conversation stopped bubbling. The visitors had left soon after dinner, not overstaying their welcome.

Later that night, Katie thought back over dinner and how nice it had been to have company over again. All four boys had gotten along well with one another.

As she got into bed, she couldn't help wondering what Mark was doing. The very next morning she would visit Pamela and find out if she'd heard anything from him.

It had been two days since Katie had talked to Pamela. In that time, Mark could've written or called Pamela.

CHAPTER 9

*There is therefore now no condemnation to them which are in
Christ Jesus, who walk not after the flesh,
but after the Spirit.*
Romans 8:1

"How was your dinner with Samuel?"

"It was nice. I think you've misjudged him. He's a nice man and his boys are lovely."

Pamela looked at her amazed. "You don't like him in that way, do you?"

"And what 'way' would that be?"

Pamela giggled. "You know what I mean. Are you thinking he would make a *gut* husband?"

"I'm not looking for a new husband, but if I were I might consider him. I think he'd be okay."

Pamela's smile faded. "You'd want someone more than okay if you're going to marry again."

"I'm feeling pressure from people to marry. Even Nathan and James want me to find a husband; I'm certain of it. They're the ones who invited Samuel over for dinner."

"You didn't tell me it was their idea."

"Jah, I did. I don't know Samuel well enough to have invited him. I wouldn't have thought of it by myself."

"Maybe you told me. *Jah*, I think you did."

"I don't have to tell you everything, do I?" Katie smiled at her friend.

"*Jah* you do have to tell me everything. I'm your best friend; who else would you tell?"

Katie sighed and didn't reply.

"Have you heard from Mark at all?" Pamela asked.

"Nee, I haven't. I thought you might have."

"Well, he called me yesterday. I just happened to be in the barn and heard the phone ring."

"What did he say?"

"He said he has the opportunity to take a job there."

This wasn't good. "He's staying there?" Katie asked trying to sound calm.

"Maybe."

"What kind of job?" Katie put her fingers to her throat. She wanted Mark to come home.

"He didn't say what kind of a job. I guess some kind of a construction job."

"What else did he say?"

"You're very interested in what he's doing."

"I am. He's always been a very good friend. He was Luke's best friend in the world; you know that."

"Is that the only reason?"

"Stop that."

"Stop what?"

"Stop doing what you're doing—implying that I like him more than as a friend."

"I don't see why you don't. You two would be perfect together."

"Let's talk about something else other than men."

"I wasn't talking about men I was talking about my *bruder*."

"You know what I mean. Stop talking about possible men for me."

"You brought it up."

Katie laughed. "I did?"

"*Jah!* You did."

"Maybe I did." Katie blew out a deep breath. "Nothing is ever easy is it?"

"I suppose not. If you think you might grow to love Mark or if there's some spark of love in your heart, I think you should do something about it now."

"Don't say any more, Pamela."

"I need to say something. I think he's ready for marriage. How would you feel if Julie snapped him up?"

"I'd be happy for him—them."

Pamela stared into her eyes. "Really?"

"*Jah*, really." Katie cleared her throat. "I want him to be happy."

"He'd be happy with you. "

"Stop it!"

Pamela laughed. "I just want *you* to be happy and not have any regrets."

"I never have regrets. I know what you're saying, but I can't marry again—not with how I felt about Luke. There's no room for another love in my heart. Luke was everything to me and just because he's not here doesn't mean I've stopped loving him. If I open my heart to anyone else it will be like I'm closing off a portion of myself. I'm not explaining it very well. Let me put it another way so you can understand. I love Luke with everything in me. And that doesn't stop just because..." Tears poured down Katie's face.

Pamela moved closer to her and put her arm around her.

"I'm so sorry for pushing Mark onto you. I guess no one knows how someone feels until they've gone through what that someone has been through. I don't know how I'd continue to breathe if I lost Micah."

Katie patted her friend's hand. "I know you're only trying to help me. And I know that you mean well. But I can't marry again. My heart forever belongs to Luke and there's no room left. I might get lonely sometimes and I know the boys would benefit from a man in their lives, and so would Lillie, but I just can't."

They sat together for a few moments in silence as they both shed tears.

"Mamma," Lillie said to her as she walked over to show her a wooden toy.

"That's lovely, Lillie, but we should go home now. Put that toy back with the others."

"You're going already?" Pamela asked.

"*Jah*, we must go. I've got to go to the markets before I collect my *kinner* from my *schweschder's haus*."

∽

Two weeks later, Lillie's birthday had come and gone, and Christmas had passed. Samuel and the boys were over at Katie's house again. They'd already eaten dinner, the boys were playing, Lillie was asleep, and Samuel and Katie were in the kitchen drinking coffee when there was a knock at the door.

"It's unusual for visitors to come so late in the night," Katie said to Samuel before she left the kitchen.

When she stepped into the room, the boys had already opened the door and wrapped their arms around the visitor, both talking at once. "Uncle Mark, are you staying?"

He talked to them in a quiet voice before he looked up at Katie. She'd nearly gasped with surprise to see Mark standing there.

"Mark, come in."

"*Denke,* Katie. How have you been?" He stepped further inside the house.

"I've been well. Have you eaten? I can fix you some dinner."

"*Nee denke.* I've eaten already. I can see by the buggy outside that you've got company."

"I've got Samuel Bontrager and his boys over for dinner."

One of the boys asked again, "Uncle Mark, are you staying?"

"I'm staying here a little while if that's all right with your *mudder.* It's just a short visit tonight."

"Are you going back to Ohio?" Nathan asked.

"I'm not sure about that yet. I'll let you know once I've made a decision."

"You boys go back and play while the adults talk in the kitchen."

Katie led Mark into the kitchen. Samuel and Mark shook hands and Katie wondered what was going on in Mark's head about Samuel being there. She desperately wanted to tell him that it wasn't what it looked like, but he didn't seem at all disturbed by seeing another man in her house.

When Katie and Mark sat down, Samuel asked Mark, "I hear you've been in Ohio?"

"*Jah.* I've been offered a job there so I'm considering going back."

"What kind of work would it be?"

"The kind of work that I do here, building. They also want me involved with the volunteer firefighters in the training department. The man they've got working on it now is about to retire."

"Who would you be working for? If you take the job?"

"The man I've been staying with for the last couple of weeks."

Katie nodded, knowing that the man he'd been staying with was Julie's younger brother. The question running through her mind was if Julie's brother had created a job to keep Mark there.

Mark looked at her and asked again, "And how have you been?"

She nodded. "I've been good."

"I'm sorry, I didn't know I'd be interrupting your dinner," he said when he looked at Samuel.

"You're not interrupting anything. We've already eaten."

Now the expression on Mark's face said it all. He obviously thought that Samuel was there for the sole purpose of making Katie his wife. She wanted to tell him that it wasn't so. But for Mark's sake maybe it was better if he thought they were becoming involved. That way Mark could make decisions without taking her and her children into account.

"Samuel's boys and mine get along really well together. They're about the same age and they're been spending a bit of time over here."

Mark then looked at Samuel who smiled back at him.

Samuel admitted, "They do get along well."

"Would you like tea or *kaffe*, Mark?"

Mark pushed out his chair. "I hadn't meant to stay. I was only coming here to tell you that I might be going back to Ohio. But I've got a few days to make a decision. I'll talk to you about it another time, Katie."

"Don't leave on my account," Samuel said. "I'll be leaving soon myself."

"*Nee* I'm not. Nice to see you again, Samuel. I'll talk to you later, Katie."

Katie walked him to the door. He stopped and said goodbye to the boys, then he quickly turned and nodded. "Goodbye, Katie."

"Why don't you drop by and see me tomorrow? I'll be home all day."

He gave a sharp nod, placed his hat on, pulled on his coat and headed out the door.

When Katie went back into the kitchen all strength left her. She just wanted to be by herself because she was feeling miserable. If Mark came by tomorrow, she didn't know if she'd be strong enough to urge him to go back to Ohio.

"How about another cup of *kaffe*?" Katie asked Samuel, not recalling whether he'd just had coffee or tea.

"I think it's about time I get the boys home."

"So soon?"

He smiled and nodded. "They'll need their sleep. With no *schul* I've got a day of chores lined up for them tomorrow."

Katie glanced at the clock on the wall. "I didn't realise how late it was."

Once the visitors had driven away in their buggy. Katie closed the door, and told her boys to brush their teeth before bed.

She was pleased that they were at an age where she no longer had to do everything for them. Katie went to her room. When she'd brushed out her hair and changed into her nightgown, she peeped into the boys' room to see them getting into bed.

"Gut nacht," she said.

They both looked up at her, and said together, *"Gut nacht, Mamm."*

She was just about to leave the room when James said, *"Mamm,* would you ever marry again?"

The question came as a shock. Didn't they remember their father? The way James asked made it sound like he wouldn't be against the idea.

"I don't think so."

"Why not? Milly's *mudder* married again, and Milly's *vadder* died when she was a *boppli.*"

She sat down on his bed while Nathan in the next bed propped himself up on his elbow.

"Some people marry again when their husband or wife dies, but some don't. It's up to the person themselves if they marry again."

"It doesn't mean you don't love *Dat* anymore," Nathan said.

"*Nee*. Milly explained it to us. She said her *mamm* said that she loved Milly's *vadder*, but she also has room in her heart to love her new husband," James said.

In a small voice, Nathan asked, "Don't you have room in your heart, *Mamm?*"

To cover up the awkwardness she felt, she laughed. "I've got loads of room in my heart. I've got room to love the three of you and all our *familye* and friends." She tickled James until he giggled.

"Tickle me," Nathan said.

She leaned over and tickled Nathan. "Now it's time for the two of you to go to sleep." She blew them each a kiss before she turned off their lantern.

Back in the bedroom that she shared with Lillie, the conversation with Nathan and James bothered her. Had they forgotten how wonderful their father was? They would have to accept the fact that her love for their father was all consuming and something never to be repeated. She would explain it to them when they were older.

She closed her bedroom door. "It's okay for Milly's *mudder*, but not for me. I'm too old to start over with a new man."

Her thoughts darted back to earlier that night and how tense it had been with both Samuel and Mark in the same room. She knew Mark would've thought that a relationship was developing between her and Samuel.

She had to make a decision whether she would have him continue to think that or let him know there was nothing going on.

Once she slipped between the covers, she tossed and turned, bothered about Mark and the idea of him going back to Ohio.

CHAPTER 10

For God so loved the world, that he gave his only begotten Son,
that whosoever believeth in him should not perish,
but have everlasting life.
John 3:16

Katie had just said goodbye to her boys as they left to play with the neighbors' children, and was sitting in the living room with Lillie when she heard a buggy. She hoped it was Mark and when she looked out the window she saw that it was. Now they could talk in private.

Katie took Lillie outside and walked over to him as he tied his horse.

He looked at her and smiled at Lillie. "Hello, you two."

"Hello, Mark." She lifted Lillie up and said to her, "You remember Uncle Mark?"

Lillie looked at him and then turned her face away. Katie placed her back on the ground.

"She doesn't remember me."

"I'm sure she does. She's just at that funny age." Katie could see that Mark was disappointed that Lillie reacted so poorly to him when the boys adored him.

"You've missed the boys; they just left to spend the day with friends."

"I'll see them at the meeting on Sunday, but it was you I came to see."

"Come inside and I'll fix us some hot tea."

Mark followed her and Lillie into the kitchen. Lillie sat down on the rug with toys while Katie put the pot on the stove to boil.

"Why do I feel like you've got something to tell me?" she asked.

"I have."

Katie sat down, joining him at the kitchen table.

"Well it's not something to tell, it's something I have to ask you."

"What is it?"

"As I mentioned last night I've been offered that job. I won't take it if you don't want me to. You know I promised Luke that I would always look after you and your *kinner.*" He paused. "It's not only that he asked me to look after you; that's not the only reason. I enjoy your company—you and the boys, and I'm sure Lillie would grow fonder of me in time."

"Of course."

He looked into her eyes. "I'm trying to tell you, Katie, that…" He breathed out heavily. "I once asked you to marry me and that still stands. Just say the word and I'll stay here as a friend and not go back to Ohio."

"I can't ask you to do that."

"You're not; I'm offering."

"I don't know what to say."

"I'll stay here as your friend or your husband whichever you'd like." He smiled at her.

She twirled the strings of her prayer *kapp* nervously around her fingers.

"I'm not very good at this sort of thing. I've never asked anyone to marry me before and now I've asked you twice."

Forcing a smile, she jumped up when she heard the water boiling. Then she poured the hot water into the teapot and placed it on the table in between them.

When she sat down again, she said, "The thing is I've made up my mind never to marry again."

"Never to marry again? Or never to marry me?" She opened her mouth to answer, but before she could, he said, "Forgive me; that wasn't fair."

"I don't know how I feel and that's the truth. You're a dear friend, but marriage must be based on more than friendship. I love you as a friend."

His shoulders drooped. "I understand. You don't need to say any more than that."

"Well I will say this, I don't want to hold you back. I want you to go and find love—find someone to marry and have your own *familye*."

"In my heart all of you are my *familye*." He glanced over at Lillie who was playing on the floor.

To stop her emotions from running away with her, she stood up and poured the tea.

"I don't really feel like hot tea," he said.

She sat back down. "Neither do I."

They both laughed.

"Why do you drink it all the time?" he asked.

"It warms me when I'm cold. I could just as easily drink hot water."

He sighed and leaned back slightly in the chair. "I hope the boys don't think I've abandoned them. I miss them terribly, but I don't want to get them too attached to me in case you marry."

"I'm not going to change my mind."

"I thought it best to tell you what's in my heart so there would be no misunderstanding between the two of us," he said.

Why couldn't things go back to how they used to be when he would come for dinner twice a week? She missed those old days when things were simpler, but nothing ever stayed the same.

AT THE NEXT SUNDAY MEETING, Mark informed Katie that he was heading back to Ohio on Wednesday.

"Can I stop by on Wednesday afternoon and say one last goodbye when I'm in the taxi heading to the bus station?"

"I'd love that." She desperately didn't want him to go.

The boys were nearby and heard what he said.

James came over to Mark. "Please don't go, Uncle Mark."

"I must go. I've got a good opportunity there."

"You can find opportunities here," James insisted.

Mark laughed. "I'll come and visit you."

"You will?" Nathan asked.

"How often?" James asked.

"Twice a year."

James mouth turned down at the corners. "That's not much."

"It's the best I can do. I'll come and say goodbye on Wednesday afternoon just after four."

Nathan said, "Maybe you'll change your mind and stay."

Mark looked directly at Katie when he said, "I don't think so."

Katie said, "Boys, I'm sure Uncle Mark needs to talk to some people and say goodbye before he goes. This will be his last meeting before he leaves. Stop hanging on to his arms and set him free."

The boys let him go.

"I'll see you on Wednesday, Katie." She nodded and then Mark looked at the boys. "You look after your *mamm*."

"We will," James said.

"We always look after her," Nathan agreed.

Mark laughed. "I'll see you on Wednesday."

Katie watched Mark walk away, and then turned back to the boys. "Come on, boys, we'll have to fetch Lillie from Pamela and go home." She glanced back over her shoulder at Mark.

∽

THE BOYS RAN to the treehouse as soon as they got home.

"Don't stay out too late," Katie called after them. "Come home well before dark. And leave your hats and coats on!"

"We will," one of the boys called back.

Katie held Lillie's hand and walked her into the house wondering what they would have for lunch. The boys had already eaten after the meeting, but she'd been too preoccupied to eat.

Just as she'd put lunch on the table, Pamela pulled up outside in the buggy. Expecting to see Pamela's whole family, she walked out the front door and was surprised to see Pamela alone.

"You're by yourself?"

"I told Micah he was in charge of the *kinner* while I

visited you." Pamela giggled. "He doesn't mind watching them."

"Come in. We're having lunch and then we can talk while Lillie has her nap."

"Does she have to nap? Can't she sit on my lap?"

"*Nee*, she gets too cranky if she misses her sleep. Have you eaten?"

"*Jah*, I ate before."

Katie guessed why Pamela was there by herself. She would've heard that Mark was going and be wanting to make sure that Katie wasn't making a mistake in not asking him to stay.

After she walked down the stairs from putting Lillie down for her nap, Katie said, "I can guess why you're here. It's about Mark."

"*Jah*, it is. Come and sit by me."

Katie sat next to her. "I'm glad you've come because I feel all mixed up."

"Tell me."

Katie gulped. "I want to be near Mark all the time, but at the same time, I can't say I want to marry him. Marriage is such a big step and when I married Luke, I married him forever."

"I know."

"Do you? I feel funny talking to you about this because Mark's your *bruder,* but you're my best friend. No one else understands me as well as you do."

"I won't repeat what you say to me."

Katie wiped a tear from her eye. "The other thing is

that he's a firefighter; what if I married him and lost him? I can't go through that again."

"Do you love him? That's the first thing you need to know and then everything else will sort itself out."

"I think I love him."

Pamela laughed. "You think?"

"It's different from the love I had for Luke. Is love different with different people? I don't know that. I don't know anything." Katie wiped her eyes.

"I'm not certain, I've only loved Micah. Maybe it is different the second time."

"I don't know what to do."

"If you love him, or if you think you love him, tell him to stay."

"I can't do that. I'm not ready for another marriage—and it would be selfish of me to hold him back while I sort out my feelings. Saying no is the only right thing to do."

"You're thinking about everybody else but yourself. What about your happiness?"

"I've had my happiness."

"When Luke was alive you mean?"

Katie nodded and nibbled on the end of her fingernail.

"Life goes on and Luke is not coming back. You've got a wonderful man and you're pretty certain you love him, so why don't you give love a chance?"

Katie shook her head. "I can't."

"*Jah,* you can. What's to stop you?"

"Mark has already put off finding a wife because of me—I'm certain of it. For the first year after Luke died, he was constantly at my *haus*."

"That's where he wanted to be."

"I know it started out because he was looking after us for Luke, but somewhere along the line we became a *familye*."

"See! You said it yourself."

Katie shook her head. "I've had love and now Mark must find someone to love him like I loved Luke."

"That person could be you if you gave yourself half a chance."

"I'm too mixed up. If I thought that, then I would tell him to stay. Half of me wants him to stay, but half of me doesn't know."

Pamela breathed out heavily. "What if you find out you love him and it's too late?"

"You mean he might find someone else?"

Pamela nodded. "Maybe."

"Then I'd be happy for him."

Pamela put her head in her hands. "You're impossible, Katie."

"I know! I've been hard for *myself* to live with. I've been in turmoil thinking of everything and wondering what I should do. But one thing my mother told me was 'when in doubt—don't.'"

"Well, I hope your *mudder* knew what she was saying."

CHAPTER 11

And above all things have fervent charity among yourselves: for charity shall cover the multitude of sins.
1 Peter 4:8

It was Wednesday, the day Mark was leaving for Ohio. Mark had told her he'd be there just after four, but it was half past four when she saw a taxi. She was relieved because she had started to think he wasn't going to say goodbye and the boys had been waiting since four.

"That's got to be him, *Mamm*."

"It seems so."

Mark got out of the taxi and the boys raced to him. He crouched down and hugged them both tightly. "I'll miss both of you."

"Don't forget to come back and see us," Nathan said.

"I won't forget."

Katie walked over to Mark holding Lillie's hand. Lillie buried her head in her mother's dress when they came close to him. He stood up and looked down into her eyes.

All she wanted was for him to wrap his arms around her like he had cuddled her boys. It wasn't an acceptable thing to do. She held out her hand, he grabbed it and held it tight while he stared into her eyes.

"Goodbye, Katie."

"Bye."

He looked down at Lillie. "Bye, Lillie."

"She's shy," Nathan said when Lillie covered her face with her hand.

Mark laughed. "She's cute." He looked back at Katie. "I'm running dreadfully late."

"Call me, or write?"

He nodded. "I will. The people I'm staying with don't have a phone in their barn, but I'll call from town."

"Who's looking after Marmalade?" Nathan asked.

"My *schweschder*, Jessie, is looking after him. She's got two dogs the same size as him. He'll be happy there."

"We could've looked after him." James looked up at his mother.

"I think your *mudder* has enough to do in looking after the three of you. Now you boys look after your *mudder*."

"We will," James said.

Nathan hugged him again.

It was upsetting for Katie to see the boys have to say goodbye to their Uncle Mark after they'd already lost their father. Mark had become a second father to them and now they were losing him, too.

He put his arms around the boys and squeezed them tight once more. "Bye, boys." He touched Lillie on her shoulder. "Bye, Lillie."

Lillie wouldn't look at him.

Mark looked back at Katie. "I'll have to go, I'm really late." He walked back to the taxi, got in and the car drove away.

The boys ran after the taxi until it was halfway down the driveway.

"I don't want him to go, *Mamm*," James said as he shuffled back toward the house.

"Neither do I," Nathan said.

"Couldn't you have married him, *Mamm*?"

Her jaw dropped open. "James, it doesn't work like that."

"Milly's *mudder*..."

"Not another word about Milly or her *mudder*—do you hear me? Not another word." She took Lillie's hand and marched into the house.

ON THE BOYS' first day back at school, Katie was cleaning up the kitchen when she heard a buggy. On looking out the window she saw it was Samuel, by himself. "That's unusual for him to visit without the boys."

She took hold of Lillie's hand and together they walked to the front door and waited for Samuel to secure his horse.

He looked over and gave her a wave when he saw them standing there. "I hope I haven't come at a bad time?"

"*Nee* I just got the boys off to *schul*."

"I've brought a box of vegetables for you. We've got more than enough and I thought you might be able to use them."

"*Denke*. I'm always able to use more food with the amount the boys are starting to eat."

He pulled a cardboard box from the back of his buggy and carried it toward her. "Where would you like it?"

"Bring it through to the kitchen, please."

Lillie and Katie followed him into the kitchen and watched him place the box on the kitchen table. Katie wondered if she should ask him for dinner now that he had brought her over a lot of vegetables. But at the same time, she didn't want to encourage him to visit too much.

"Would you and the boys be free for dinner tonight?" She thought it only polite to ask.

"I can't tonight I've got a meeting with the bishop."

"Okay. Thank you for bringing all this wonderful food. She looked at the pumpkins, the squash and the zucchini. I don't know how you can grow things in the cold weather."

"I grow them under cover to keep them warm."

"At least stay and have a cup of hot tea with me, won't you?"

"I would love a cup of *kaffe*. If you have something with me?"

"I'm always ready for a cup of tea."

"And how are you today, Lillie?"

"*Gut,*" she answered.

"That's *gut.*" Samuel laughed, and said to Katie, "She's speaking well isn't she?"

"*Jah.* It helps having two brothers who are constantly talking." When she'd made him the coffee, she said, "Would you care to sit out on the porch? We can enjoy the sun while it's shining."

"*Jah,* let me carry that out for you."

Katie thought it best to sit on the porch even if it was rather cool. There had been talk about her and Mark, so it wouldn't do to have talk circulating about her and another man. Not too much could be made of things if they were talking on the porch rather than inside the house. Katie placed her daughter on a chair in between herself and Samuel; she felt safer that way somehow.

After Samuel took a mouthful of coffee, he said, "Katie, have you ever considered marrying again?"

She had considered it only because Mark had suggested that he marry her, but she didn't want Samuel to know that. "That's a hard subject for me to talk about."

"That makes it hard for me to ask my next question."

"Just ask me. What is it?"

He took a large mouthful of coffee. "Wowee! That's hot."

"Would you like some cold water in it, or some milk perhaps?"

"*Nee*, that's okay. I just need to be more patient."

"Are you sure?" She would've liked to have a little break from this conversation because she was pretty sure she knew what he was going to ask her and that would be very awkward for both of them.

"I want to ask you to marry me. Will you marry me, Katie?"

The only thing she was able to do was look down at her daughter and pull her coat around her better. She couldn't look Samuel in the face. The man deserved to know how she felt; she wouldn't mislead him. "Samuel, I will never marry again. I was married to Luke for so many years and had three children with him. Well, two children with him and he didn't even get to find out

Lillie was on her way into the world. I could never marry again. I'm certain I told you that."

He looked down at the boards on the porch. "I had to ask." He gave a little laugh.

"I feel honoured that you would think of me in such a way."

"I do; I think very highly of you."

"We will always be friends."

"*Jah*, we'll always be friends."

Samuel looked at her and smiled. "I can never have too many friends." He looked down at Lillie and then started talking to Lillie about the cookie she was crumbling into her dress.

CHAPTER 12

Fear thou not; for I am with thee: be not dismayed; for I am thy God: I will strengthen thee; yea, I will help thee; yea, I will uphold thee with the right hand of my righteousness.
Isaiah 41:10

Winter turned into spring and then summer, and Katie hadn't heard a word from Mark in six months. She'd hardly heard any news of him from Pamela, so it was odd that Mark would suddenly decide to write to her.

She stared down at the letter from Mark, and then held it up to the light. A letter dated six months from the day he left could only mean that he was telling her that he was getting married. Pamela had mentioned nothing, but perhaps Mark wanted her to hear it from him first rather than from another person. Mark was thoughtful like that.

The notion of him getting married churned at her stomach in a most uncomfortable way.

Katie hid the letter away from her children by putting it in the top shelf of the utility room off from the kitchen. The shelf was too high for them to see and if they saw an unopened letter from their Uncle Mark they would think it strange. The last thing she wanted to do was answer any difficult questions.

She tried to put the letter out of her mind, but the possible content of it was nagging at her. What if Mark had found somebody he wanted to marry? She'd have to be happy for him, but sadness gnawed at her stomach.

It was two nights later that Samuel and his two boys were over for dinner. She'd forgotten that the letter was in the utility room when she asked Samuel to fetch salt for her. Along with the salt, he returned with Mark's letter.

She looked at it and then looked up at Samuel's confused face. "I'm so absent minded lately. That's where the letter got to; I've been looking for it." After Katie had plucked the letter from his hands, she placed it on the kitchen sink.

"Aren't you going to open it?" Samuel asked.

THE AMISH FIREFIGHTER'S WIDOW

"*Nee,* I'll read it later. It won't be anything important. Just a letter."

"Does he often write to you?"

She shook her head. Samuel seemed too interested in the letter for her liking. And after dinner that night she was to find out why.

Lillie was in bed and the four boys were playing a game in the living room when Samuel said he had something important to discuss with her.

"Come and I'll make us a cup of tea in the kitchen," Katie said.

Once they were seated with tea, she asked, "What's on your mind?"

"Our boys get along well together and I've got—grown fond of you and your *kinner.* I was wondering if we might join our households. I know you told me you would never marry, but if we do it for practical purposes it might make more sense to you and make our lives easier."

She frowned not wanting to have to turn him down once more. "I'm sure I told you a long time ago and just recently how I felt about a second marriage."

"You did. But I was hoping that you might have changed your mind. I think *Gott* meant for people not to be alone."

"I can't, Samuel. I just can't. For so many reasons—I can't."

He nodded. "I understand. I thought I should at least try to change your mind. I didn't want to lose you or have you choose someone else thinking that I was no longer keen on marrying you. If I can ask you why haven't you opened that letter from Mark?"

"Why, have you heard something? Is there something wrong with Mark? Is he ill?"

"I haven't heard anything of the kind. I've heard nothing about him since he left."

Katie's forehead furrowed into a frown. "I'll open the letter later."

"It seems you might be hiding your feelings for a certain man."

"*Nee*, I'm not at all; it's not like that. Mark was Luke's very best friend."

"Luke's not coming back and Mark remains. Is that any reason to punish the man?"

"What do you mean?"

"Any reason to punish Mark?"

"I'm not at all. I think there's been some misunderstanding." She sipped on her tea while thinking how she should change the subject.

He nodded. "It's not my business, but I do care about you and the boys and if you're not going to marry me, you should marry someone."

"I thought we talked about this some time ago," she muttered, wanting the conversation to end.

"We did."

"I'm sorry, Samuel, I just can't talk about this anymore."

"Okay. I won't talk about marriage or Mark again." He smiled at her. "I didn't mean to distress you."

"That's okay. You didn't—not too much."

"As soon as I drink this, I'll get the boys home. It's getting late."

Katie smiled back at him. She liked the company of him and his boys, but not when he was pressuring her about marriage.

LATER THAT NIGHT when Katie was back in her bedroom and Lillie was sound asleep, she decided it was time to read the letter. Pulling on her dressing gown, she headed to the kitchen. She grabbed the letter and raced back upstairs hoping she wouldn't wake the boys.

Once she was back to her bedroom, she carefully peeled the envelope open by the light of the kerosene lamp. She smelled the letter, hoping to smell Mark's familiar scent, but all she smelled was paper.

At that moment she hoped with all her heart that he wasn't getting married. Even though she knew she was being selfish, it would make her heart ache to hear such news.

Once she unfolded the page, she scanned the letter from top to bottom looking for the words marry or married. When she saw nothing of the kind, she read the letter from the beginning. He explained how he'd been too sad to come and visit them because if he came he wouldn't want to leave. Mark went on to ask her to say hello to the boys and said he would see them soon, before Christmas, but only if she said she wanted him back. Otherwise he would stay on in Ohio.

"Before Christmas," she said out loud. "He can't do this. The boys will be so disappointed." At least, Mark wasn't getting married. Pleased that the letter said nothing of a woman or of marriage, she read the letter again.

At the bottom of the letter, he'd mentioned he would return and stay for good if she wanted him to come back. It would feel odd to marry again—and that's what she knew Mark meant.

If she asked him to come back and things didn't work out between them she would never be able to forgive herself. She'd found love once in her life, and she wouldn't stop Mark from finding it. She decided not to write back, and left everything in God's hands.

CHAPTER 13

Confess your faults one to another, and pray one for another, that ye may be healed. The effectual fervent prayer of a righteous man availeth much.
James 5:16

It was three years to the day since Luke had died. Katie wanted to visit Luke's grave. The boys were at school and she'd left Lillie at her sister's house. She pulled up in the buggy and parked it as close as she could, but still, his grave was over at the other side of the yard. As she walked, she mentally rehearsed everything she'd say to him—what was going on in her life and the boys' lives and how fast Lillie was growing.

When she looked up to see how much further she

had to walk, there was a tall man standing over the grave. She stopped in her tracks. The man looked like Mark. Was it Mark? Chills ran through her body as she watched him. The man slowly turned and she saw that it was Mark.

She collapsed on the ground as tears poured down her face. She hadn't seen him or heard from him since she'd gotten that letter. It was as though two worlds had collided, and she was right in the middle when they had.

Mark ran to her and pulled her to her feet. She wrapped her arms around him and held him tight, never wanting to let go. Slowly and tenderly he placed his arms around her and held her.

After a couple of minutes passed, he pulled back. "Are you okay?"

With tears still streaming down her face, she nodded. "I'm okay."

She picked up the end of her apron and dabbed her eyes.

"Why the tears? Is everything all right?"

She sniffed. "Everything's okay. I've missed you, that's all." She put her arms around him again and buried her face into his shoulder, never wanted him to leave. But what if he had returned to tell everyone he was getting married?

Katie stepped back. "Why are you here?"

"Do you know what day it is?"

"Luke died three years ago today, that's what day

it is."

"I came here because I thought you'd come. I was waiting for you. The truth is, I want to talk to you in private. Well, in private, but in front of Luke." He smiled and she laughed a little.

"What did you want to talk to me about?"

"*Nee.* I can't say now. It's probably a mistake me coming here."

"*Nee,* it wasn't." She swallowed hard. It was her turn to show him her interest and be truthful about what was in her heart. "Do you still want to marry me?"

His soft brown eyes crinkled at the corners. "I've never stopped wanting to marry you. Have you realized after so long that you're in love with me?"

She dipped her head. "It took a long time for me to admit that I love you. It's not easy having so many feelings in my head and in my heart and…"

"I understand."

"Do you?"

He laughed. "*Nee,* I don't think I do, but I'm trying to understand." He took both of her hands in his. "I've always liked you as a good friend when you were married, but now I can't see myself with anybody but you." He cleared his throat and continued, "I was hoping and praying that you would feel the same one day soon."

"I do feel the same; it's taken me awhile to see it. I think it took you going away and being out of my life to know that I don't ever want you to leave me again."

"I won't, Katie, I won't." He pulled her in close, and once again, she
buried her face into his shoulder.

"When you wrote me that letter, I couldn't open it for days. I was frightened that the letter would say you were getting married. It was then I began to understand my true feelings."

"Only then?"

"I think so."

After a few moments, Mark said, "What do you think Luke would think about us being together?"

"I know in my heart he would be happy. You would be the best choice. If he could choose anyone, I know he'd put me with you."

"*Denke,*" he said softly. "That makes me feel so much better. And does that mean that you'll marry me?"

"I will, of course, I will."

"*Denke, Katie, denke.*"

"There are no words to describe how happy the boys will be about this. They've missed you so much and they would love to have you there every day."

"And I'll get to know Lillie."

Katie giggled. "She's a little shy."

"So it's not just me, then?"

Katie shook her head. "*Nee.* She's like that with everybody. She turns her head away; she's just going through an awkward stage."

"Katie, I don't want to waste any more time. We've

already wasted enough. I want us to get married as soon as we can. I'll visit the bishop today and tell him we want to get married."

"*Jah*, I agree I think we need to be together as soon as possible."

"I guess the bishop will want to see both of us together. I'll make an appointment for us."

"That would be good, Mark."

"Why don't I let you talk to Luke in private and I'll see you later today?"

"*Jah*. Come by when the boys are home, they'll be so excited to see you. I don't think we should mention getting married, though, until we've spoken to the bishop."

"Yes, of course, that would be best. You won't change your mind, will you?"

She shook her head and smiled.

"Is there something on your mind? You seem quiet."

She rubbed her forehead. "What if I lose you the same way I lost Luke? You're a firefighter just like he was."

"You'll lose me one day, or I'll lose you. Neither one of us is going to live forever."

She looked down at the ground. "I know that. It's just that I don't know if I can go through that again."

"You might never have to, but isn't it better to be happy rather than fearful? The choice is yours. Be happy that we're together and if tragedy strikes again one day, know that it's *Gott's* will and He will be there for you to turn to."

Katie nodded. "You're right."

"Otherwise you'll deny yourself happiness through fear." He laughed. "I might die a cranky old man and you'll have no peace until I finally breathe my last breath."

She laughed. "I hope you die an old man. That will mean I'll have you longer."

"We have hope, we have love, and we have it all."

She nodded again.

"Now, I'll leave you alone to be with Luke, and I'll drop by at the house later and say hello to the boys. Then I'll have to try to get Lillie to see that I'm okay."

"That sounds good."

He pulled her to him one more time and pressed his lips lightly on her forehead before he let her go.

Katie watched him leave and saw that his buggy had been tied to a tree on the outer side of the graveyard. Once he drove away, she leaned down and picked up the blanket she'd dropped when she'd seen Mark. She spread out the blanket by Luke's grave and sat down.

"I suppose you saw and heard it all. I hope you are okay with me marrying Mark. It seems strange that I loved you, still do and always will, but now I love him also. It's not something I ever considered would happen. I tried my best not to love him; there was only room for you in my heart. I guess *Gott* worked to open my heart to love again."

CHAPTER 14

Beloved, I wish above all things that thou mayest prosper and be in health, even as thy soul prospereth.
3 John 1:2

Katie left Luke's grave feeling free. Before, she'd been living in fear, but now she'd admitted her feelings about Mark and she felt like a load had lifted off her shoulders. She collected Lillie from her sister's house and when they got home, Lillie was ready for a nap.

Once Lillie was asleep, Katie prayed. She thanked God for the two wonderful men he'd blessed her with. It was nice that the two men she'd loved in her lifetime had enjoyed such a close bond. That way, she knew

Luke would've approved of Mark being her second husband.

Katie headed to the kitchen to get the evening meal underway hoping that Mark would join them for dinner just like he used to.

It wasn't long after that, that Katie heard the boys laughing and talking as they rode up on their bikes, having finished school. As usual they placed their bikes in the barn and ran into the house.

"Boys, I'm always telling you not to run indoors."

A breathless Nathan said, "Sorry, *Mamm*."

"*Jah*, sorry, *Mamm*."

She stood in front of them with her hands on her hips. "I've got a surprise for you today."

"Are we having eggs for dinner?" James asked.

She laughed. "Even better than that."

"I can smell roast chicken. Is someone coming for dinner?" Nathan asked.

"*Jah*. Someone you like very much is coming for dinner. He's coming soon, but we must ask him if he'll stay for dinner."

"Uncle Mark?" Nathan asked.

"*Jah!*"

The boys jumped up and down while they squealed with delight.

"He's coming over here to see you boys and we'll have to ask nicely if he'll stay for dinner. Maybe he's got other plans, but if he doesn't I'm certain he'll stay."

"We'll make him stay won't we, Nathan?"

"*Jah,* we'll ask him very nicely if he'll stay for dinner, and then we won't let him leave."

"*Mamm!*" Lillie called from upstairs.

"Nathan, can you go up and get your *schweschder?*"

"I'll go and get her," James said. Both boys ran upstairs.

Katie was excited to see the boys so pleased about their Uncle Mark coming to visit. She and Mark would have to wait until they spoke to the bishop before they told anyone, even the boys, the good news.

Once the boys had brought Lillie into the kitchen, they asked Katie more questions.

"Is he staying here or going back to Ohio?" James asked.

"I'll let you boys ask him that."

"That sounds like he's staying," James said.

"Like I said, you'll have to ask him."

"That makes me very happy," Nathan said. "I never wanted him to go to Ohio in the first place."

"Will he bring Marmalade with him?" James asked.

"I don't know. We'll have to wait and see."

"I'm hungry, *Mamm,*" Lillie said.

"Me too," James said.

"Me three." Nathan laughed at himself.

Katie hadn't seen the boys this happy for some time. "Everyone sit down at the table and I'll fix you something to eat. After that, you boys can go into your room and clean it."

"Our room is so tidy already, *Mamm,*" James said.

"It might be tidy, but it's not clean, not by my standards."

"There's no use arguing with her," Nathan whispered to his older brother.

"Yeah, you're right," James whispered back. "After we clean our room can we go out and play, *Mamm?*"

Just as James had spoken, they heard a buggy. The boys rushed to the window.

"It's Uncle Mark!" James yelled before both boys ran out of the house.

Katie looked out the kitchen window to see the boys hugging Mark. She turned to Lillie. "Come, let's see Uncle Mark."

Lillie slid off the chair and took her mother's hand, and together they walked out to the porch.

Nathan came rushing back toward Katie. "He's stayin', he's stayin'!"

"*Wunderbaar!*" Katie said as she looked at Nathan's face all flushed with excitement. She looked up at Mark and he smiled at her. "Can you stay for dinner, Mark?"

"*Jah,* stay, stay," James and Nathan chorused.

He laughed. "I'd love to stay."

"*Gut!*" Katie said.

Nathan tugged on his arm. "Will you play with us now, Uncle Mark?"

"If that's all right with your *mudder?*"

"Is it, *Mamm?*" James asked.

"*Jah.* You boys do what you will and Lillie and I'll

see to the dinner. It'll be about an hour and a half away."

As she walked back to the kitchen with Lillie, she thought about how long the bishop would make them wait to marry. Maybe they'd have to wait two or three months. The moment they were alone she would ask Mark if he'd already made a time to see the Bishop.

CHAPTER 15

A merry heart doeth good like a medicine: but a broken spirit drieth the bones.
Proverbs 17:22

It was only two days later that they both sat before Bishop John in his house.

Bishop John sat in front of them stroking his long gray beard as he announced he was going to ask them questions. The first question took Katie by surprise.

"Why do you want to marry each other now, after all this time that you've known each other?"

Katie's jaw dropped open and she looked at Mark who spoke for her. "It took some time for Katie to know she wasn't disrespecting Luke."

"That's right." Katie looked over at the bishop. "I've

had so many feelings about the whole thing of loving again. At first it felt like betrayal—like I was betraying Luke."

The bishop shook his head. "Many widows believe this, but once they marry again the previous married life fades; you concentrate on your new husband. Marrying again, Katie, doesn't mean you'll never be sad, nor does it mean that you won't miss Luke."

Katie nodded.

The bishop continued in his slow deliberate way of speaking, "You don't have to be alone forever. You didn't choose for Luke to leave you alone, yet here you are before me a widow at a comparatively young age. Nothing you could have done would've changed what *Gott* had set in place before time began." He looked at Mark. "Mark, you must understand that there is a place in Katie's heart always for Luke, but it's in the past. You must learn to honor that."

"I understand that," Mark said. "I loved him, too."

"Katie, you must not live in the past. You can love your past, but not live in something that no longer exists. You should not love your past so much that you want to remain in it. None of us can do that. We must treasure what *Gott* gives us daily—not looking to the future or to the past."

"That makes sense," Katie said wondering why she hadn't visited the bishop and talked to him sooner.

"With regard to love, our hearts are without limits,

just as *Gott's* love is limitless. Katie, I'm sure you love all your *kinner* and not just one of them."

Katie smiled and gave a little nod knowing where he was going with that line of thinking.

"When you marry Mark, it won't mean that you're forgetting Luke or the life that you shared together. Marrying for a second time does not mean that you're wiping away the love or the life you had with Luke."

"It makes me feel better just talking with you," Katie said. "But if Luke was still alive, I wouldn't have fallen in love with Mark. That's something that keeps nagging at the back of my mind. Mark would've just been a friend and I find that an odd thing to think about."

"Don't think about it, then," Mark said.

The bishop leaned back. "What does the bible say about remarriage, you might ask?"

Katie shook her head, knowing that the bishop could talk for many hours once he got started quoting scriptures. "We didn't ask, I think we know…"

"Here's what it says." His eyes lifted up to the ceiling as he said, "In chapter seven of 1 Corinthians: *I say therefore to the unmarried and widows, it is good for them if they abide even as I. But if they cannot contain, let them marry: for it is better to marry than to burn.*"

Katie felt her cheeks turn crimson, and she hoped the bishop didn't think that either she or Mark was lustful.

"More importantly, we know from chapter 7 of

Romans, and I will quote it: *For the woman which hath an husband is bound by the law to her husband so long as he liveth; but if the husband be dead, she is loosed from the law of her husband. So then if, while her husband liveth, she be married to another man, she shall be called an adulteress: but if her husband be dead, she is free from that law; so that she is no adulteress, though she be married to another man.* Death is all that can break the marriage vows, in *Gott's* sight."

Katie breathed out heavily. She knew all of these things.

"Now had you come to me within weeks of Luke's death then I would've had concerns about the pair of you. Katie, I would've thought you were covering up the pain of your loss with a hasty marriage. Mark, you might have been coveting your neighbor's wife."

Mark's mouth turned down at the corners and he was about to speak when the bishop jumped back in.

"But now, years on, it seems the two of you have had a *gut* long time to think about what you're about to do."

"You mean marriage?" Mark asked.

"*Jah*, you've both taken the time to think things through."

"We have. We've had a long time to think. Especially when Mark was in Ohio."

"Sometimes distance between a couple can prove useful," the bishop said with a smile.

The bishop's wife, Mavis, came in with a tray of tea

and cake and said to her husband, "Are you going away somewhere, dear?"

"*Nee*, I was speaking in general about couples. Did you want a break from me?" he asked with a smile.

"We've never had time away from each other," Mavis told Mark and Katie.

"We haven't finished our talk," the bishop said, frowning as his wife placed the tray on the coffee table.

Mavis said, "I think you must be ready for some tea by now."

The bishop said, "We've only just started!"

"Perhaps we might take a break?" Mark suggested. "Just so we can absorb all the words of wisdom we've just heard."

"I suppose a break might serve a purpose." He glanced up at his wife again. *"Denke,* Mavis."

"I'll get some small plates for the cake." Mavis disappeared from the room.

"So, when is the soonest we can marry?"

"I'm not going to delay the pair of you for any reason if that's what you want to know," the bishop said to Mark.

Katie smiled and looked at Mark who smiled back. The first person she wanted to tell, after her children, was Pamela.

CHAPTER 16

But love ye your enemies, and do good, and lend, hoping for nothing again; and your reward shall be great, and ye shall be the children of the Highest: for he is kind unto the unthankful and to the evil.

Luke 6:35

Katie had never been able to throw out any of her late husband's belongings, but now was the time to do so. Wanting to be alone while she sorted through Luke's things, she'd taken Lillie to her sister's place. Now she was back home in her bedroom and just about to begin the cleansing process.

The first things were the love letters he'd sent her. When she opened the cardboard box that hadn't been opened for years, she saw around fifty letters. Tears streamed down her face and she couldn't throw the letters away. Surely Mark wouldn't mind if she kept the letters in a box at the back of one of the drawers in the bedroom. It was part of her history and part of her life. And part of her children's history.

After wiping her tears away and tucking the box into the back of a drawer, she sorted through all his clothes that were still in their room. All his clothes would go to charity, but she would keep one of his shirts. She opened the top drawer of her chest of drawers and reached to the back and pulled out a white handkerchief. After she'd unfolded it she saw that it was still there, but now dried and crumpled—the daisy he'd given her on their first buggy ride together when they were courting. She added it to the box of letters.

∽

ONCE SHE HAD SORTED through Luke's things, she went to Pamela's. Mark had said she could tell her first.

"Do you know Mark has come back here to live?" Pamela asked.

"*Jah.*"

"So you've seen him?"

"I have."

"Why are you smiling like that? Have you two sorted out your differences?" Pamela asked.

"We never had any differences."

"You know what I mean."

Katie laughed.

"Now I know something's going on. You two have talked haven't you? What came out of it?"

"That's what I'm here to tell you."

A look of delight ran across Pamela's face. "Tell me quick."

"Mark asked me to marry him."

Pamela opened her mouth and squealed so loud that Katie had to cover her ears.

"I hope you accepted," she asked suddenly.

"You didn't let me finish. Yes, I accepted."

Pamela jumped up and down. "I'm so pleased." She hugged Katie tightly, then released her. "Do you know this makes us…well, you'll be my *schweschder*-in-law."

"I just realized that too." Katie laughed.

"This is the best news I've heard since I don't know when. Tell me all about it. How did he ask you?"

"I can't tell you that. That's personal."

Pamela giggled. "When are you getting married?"

"We're getting married in eight weeks."

"I can't believe it. I just can't believe it. He's already spoken to the bishop, then?"

"*Jah* we spoke to him just last night and the first person I wanted to tell was you."

"Have you told the boys yet?"

"We're telling them tonight together. We're going to tell them over dinner."

"Can I tell Micah?"

"*Jah,* but he'll have to keep it quiet until it's published."

"And where will you live?"

"We haven't discussed it."

"You're probably going to need a bigger *haus* now. Have you still got Lillie in with you?"

"*Jah.*"

"That won't do. And the boys are still sharing a room?"

"*Jah.* I suppose we are going to need a least one more bedroom. Unless Lillie squashes in with the boys for a while."

"And then you have to keep adding on every time you have another *boppli.*"

"If the Lord blesses us with *kinner.*"

"And why wouldn't He? He's already blessed you with a second husband. You must've gotten over your apprehension about marrying another firefighter."

"I think so. Mark said to me there's no use worrying about things that might never happen, and he's right."

"Of course he's right."

"It's taken me a long time, but I'm finally ready; the time seems right. I'm just glad that Mark was patient and waited for me."

"He loves you that much, that's why he waited."

"I guess he does."

"What did the bishop say? Was he surprised?"

"*Nee,* he didn't seem surprised at all. He was mainly focused on telling me that I shouldn't feel bad for marrying again. I don't know how he knew what was on my mind. It made me regret not going to speak to him long ago. I don't know how he got the wisdom of all those things he said to me. We were there for hours while he went on and on and going over scriptures. I think that Mark was getting a little bored, but everything the bishop said gave me answers to all my questions."

"I guess that's why the Lord chose him as the bishop. He hears the word and the thoughts of *Gott;* maybe that's how he knew exactly what to say to you."

"That must be right because he's only had the one marriage himself. I don't know how he would've known some of the things he said unless he'd talked to other women about how they felt."

"Other widows you mean?"

"Jah."

"I'm just so happy for you. I always thought you two would be great together and seems like I was right."

"I wouldn't have felt right to marry him any earlier, but now I feel that it's time to move forward. It doesn't mean that I love Luke any less."

"Of course it doesn't. No one would ever think that."

CHAPTER 17

Not rendering evil for evil, or railing for railing: but contrariwise blessing; knowing that ye are thereunto called, that ye should inherit a blessing.
1 Peter 3:9

As usual, Katie heard the boys coming home from school before she saw them. They were hollering and laughing as they rode their bikes toward the house. Lillie was awake and ran out to meet them. Katie was just about to tell them that Mark was coming to dinner when she saw Mark's buggy approaching.

"Look who's coming, boys," she called out to them, pointing at the buggy.

The boys turned to see Mark and their faces lit up.

"Great! It's Uncle Mark."

"Let's go and show him the tree *haus* and what we've done with it," James said to Nathan.

"*Jah.*"

They waited until the buggy stopped and they rushed to Mark.

Mark looked over at Katie. "It looks like I'm going for a walk to the tree *haus.*"

"Take your time; dinner is still a couple of hours away."

"Can I go too?" Lillie asked.

"Boys come and get your *schweschder;* she wants to go with you."

James ran back and grabbed Lillie's hand and hurried, at Lillie's pace, to join Nathan and Mark who were already walking away. Katie felt as though she had a real family again. With Mark and her three children her family was complete.

When Katie walked back into the house, she realized she hadn't given the boys anything to eat. They always ate as soon as they got home from school. "That means they'll be extra hungry for dinner," she said to herself.

Lamb chops with loads of vegetables were on the menu. Lamb chops were Mark's favorite, and everyone liked mashed potatoes.

WHILE THEY WERE EATING DINNER, Mark told the boys that he was staying in Lancaster County. He'd forgotten that the boys had already heard that.

"Well, I've got something that you don't know already," Mark said with his brown eyes twinkling.

Nathan stopped eating and looked at him. "What's that, Uncle Mark?"

Mark looked across at Katie. "Do you want to tell them, or shall I?"

Katie giggled. "You can tell them."

Both boys stared at him.

Mark took a moment, and then said, "Your *mudder* has agreed to marry me."

"Wait a minute. For real?" Nathan said.

"Is this a joke?" James asked, looking at his mother and then back at Mark.

Mark laughed. "I wouldn't joke about something this important. We're getting married. What do you say? Are you happy?"

The boys jumped out of their seats and didn't know what to do with themselves.

"Getting married for real? That means you'll live with us every day and you won't leave us again?" James asked.

"I will never leave any of you again. I'll always be here for all of you."

Lillie was too interested in the food and kept eating.

The boys threw their arms around Mark and nearly tipped him off his chair.

"That was a good idea, *Mamm,* to marry Uncle Mark. Wait a minute. Will we have to call you *Dat?*" James asked.

"You can call me *Dat* or Uncle Mark or think of something better. I guess maybe your *mudder* and I will have to talk about it."

"Lillie never knew *Dat.*" Nathan started crying and James leaned over and patted his brother's back.

James said, "It's alright, Nathan. It's easier for her that way."

Katie didn't expect that they would've talked about their father when they learned she would marry Mark. It had taken her by surprise; this was not how she'd pictured things going. Seeing her youngest son cry caused tears to form in her eyes. She dabbed at her tears with a napkin.

James looked at her. "Don't cry, *Mamm.*"

"I cry all the time," she said not wanting them to read too much into her tears.

"Girls cry all the time," Nathan said through sniffs.

"I wouldn't say that's true," Katie said. "Now eat up your food."

"When is the wedding? Tomorrow?" James asked.

"Today?" Nathan said with a huge grin.

"In a few weeks time," Mark answered.

After a while Nathan asked, "Are we all gonna live here or are we gonna move into a bigger better *haus?*"

"I didn't know you two would have so many questions," Katie said.

"Your *mudder* and I haven't talked about where we're going to live. When we've figured it out we'll let you know. My *haus* is too small, but then this one is too. Too small for the five of us."

"We'll figure it out," Katie said.

∽

THE NIGHT before Katie's wedding, she reread all of Luke's letters. Now that she'd read them, she wouldn't want to pick them up for a long time. She was moving on; Luke was her past and Mark was her future. Then she went to bed and slept well, knowing that her future was in *Gott's* hands.

As she opened her eyes to greet the morning, she knew that she was on a journey where she was growing and learning about herself and about God. The wedding was to be held at her older sister's house because her house wouldn't have fitted half of the guests that would be coming. She and Mark had decided to sell both of their houses and buy a bigger one. In the meantime, they would live in her house and Lillie would move into the boys' room.

"Wake up, *Mamm*, you're getting married today!"

She looked over at the door to see the boys staring at her. "What's the time?"

"It's six o'clock," James said.

"I told you we don't have to wake up until seven."

Nathan said, "We didn't want you to be late."

"I'll never be late with you two boys around."

The boys laughed.

"You get ready and I'll dress Lillie, then I'll go down and get the breakfast started."

The boys hurried away.

Anne, Katie's sister, arrived just before seven to take the children back to her place. Shortly after that, Pamela arrived. Pamela was to be Katie's attendant.

"Are you nervous?" Pamela asked.

"I'm excited. This is the start of a new chapter of my life. I'm pleased. I feel I've been through the dark years and now I'm hoping I can have some light in my life."

"You deserve every piece of happiness you get."

"*Denke*, Pamela."

"I mean it."

"I hope so."

Both women laughed.

Katie looked down at her dark blue dress. "*Denke* for making this dress for me. You were always so much better at sewing than I was."

"You look lovely in it. It brings out your eyes."

"I suppose we should leave now."

"*Jah*, you should be married in about an hour."

Katie giggled. "The way bishop John talks it will be more like two hours."

Pamela smiled. "He does get onto a roll sometimes when he gets started."

An hour later, Mark and Katie were standing before the bishop. The minister had given a short talk followed by William Hostetler who sang a hymn in High German. The bishop went into a lengthy explanation about marriage and how it was a representation of Christ and the body of Christ, which was His church. Finally, Mark and Katie were pronounced man and wife.

They smiled as they gazed into each other's eyes. The kiss would wait until they were alone. They held hands and walked out of the house to the wedding reception area that was set up in the yard.

As they wandered to the table, Mark said, *"Denke* for marrying me, Katie. You've made me the happiest man who ever walked the earth."

She laughed. "I'm glad. You deserve to be happy, Mark. You're truly the nicest man I know."

CHAPTER 18

My little children, let us not love in word, My little children, let us not love in word, neither in tongue; but in deed and in truth.

1 John 3:18

It was four months after their wedding and two months after they'd moved into their new house, and Katie had some exciting news to give her husband. She'd kept the news to herself for days so she could tell him on his birthday.

On his birthday, she woke up alone. He'd been called to a fire during the night. When she saw that he still wasn't home, she got worried. She jumped out of bed and wrapped herself in a bathrobe and hurried out to the barn to use the phone. When she found Pamela's number she called it, since Micah, Pamela's husband was also a volunteer firefighter.

"He's not home yet. Why?"

"I thought they should've been home by now, too. Don't worry. I'm sure everything's all right."

"What was the location of the fire?"

"I'll just have a look to see if Micah wrote it down." A minute later, Pamela was back on the line and gave Katie the address.

Katie hung up the phone after she'd scribbled the address down. The next thing she did was call a taxi. Thankfully, she remembered she was in a robe, so she sprinted to the house to get changed as fast as she could.

Before she left the house, she woke James and told him to look after the others and stay in the house until she got back. The shrill horn of the taxi rang in her ears.

"What's wrong, *Mamm?*"

"Nothing. I've just got to go somewhere."

"Where's Pa?"

James and his younger brother had decided before their mother's wedding that the best name for Uncle Mark was Pa.

"He was called out in the middle of the night to a fire. I've got to go now." Katie hurried out to the taxi and gave the driver the address she'd scribbled out. She had no idea how far away it was. It had to be in the vicinity somewhere; otherwise Mark and Micah wouldn't have been called out.

"How far away is it?" she asked the driver.

"About fifteen minutes."

"Can you hurry?"

"I'll go as fast as I can."

She slid down in the back seat worried that it was happening all over again.

"Looks like there's been a fire," the taxi driver said as he pulled up behind one of the fire trucks.

"This is the place. Thank you." She handed the money over and then jumped out of the car. As she got closer she saw the devastation that the fire had created. Trying to calm herself she walked on further. It was then that she saw some blackened firefighters who were drinking soda from cans. It seemed they'd been taking it in shifts.

"Katie!"

She looked at the group of men again, and from among them Mark emerged. Tears rolled down her face and he ran toward her.

"What is it?" He held both of her shoulders and stared down into her face.

She shook her head. "You're all right."

He pulled her close.

"Careful, don't get my dress dirty. You're covered in black."

"I'm sorry. I should've called, but I thought it was too early. I didn't want to wake you and you probably wouldn't even be able to hear the phone. It looks like we'll be here for a few more hours. You know these things can take a long time."

"I know, but when you weren't there when I woke up, I thought the worst. It's your birthday and I had been saving something to tell you. When you weren't there, I was scared and then I thought you'd never know what I had to tell you."

"What's wrong?"

She shook her head again. "Nothing's wrong. I feel foolish now coming out here like this."

"You should never feel foolish, ever."

She sniffed.

"What did you have to tell me that was so important?"

She looked at the men talking in the group near the truck. It wasn't the ideal place to tell him, but she was there now and she didn't want to wait any longer. "I found out a couple of days ago, but I thought it would be a nice surprise for your birthday."

"You're getting the children a puppy?"

She shook her head.

"Me a puppy? I don't know how Marmalade would feel about that."

"*Nee, nee,* nothing like that." She looked down at her stomach and placed her hand over her belly, then looked up at him and smiled.

"You're not, are you?"

She nodded. "I am. We're having a *boppli.*"

His eyes filled with tears as his hand flew to his mouth. Then he covered his face with his hands. It was a moment before he could speak. "I never thought it would happen this quickly. I mean, I hoped that one day we might have a *boppli*, but... What shall we tell the boys and Lillie?"

She laughed. "We'll tell them we're having a *boppli* and they'll soon have a new *bruder* or *schweschder*."

"We're on again in ten, Mark," one of the men in the group called out.

"Okay," he called back over his shoulder. He looked back at Katie and held her hand then brought it to his lips and kissed it. "I don't know when I'll be home, but I must stay here."

"I know."

"You go home and wait, and please, don't worry. It's bad to worry in your condition."

She sniffled. "I know. I feel better now that I've seen you and told you the news."

He smiled and pulled her into his arms. "I love you, Katie. I'll have someone call you a taxi. I don't want you breathing in this smoky air."

When Katie was back home again, she felt fine. All anxiousness had left her.

The boys came running out as she pulled the front door open.

"Where did you go, *Mamm?*" James asked.

"I had to see Pa just quickly. He was at a fire. I had to tell him something."

"That you love him?" Nathan laughed.

She smiled. "Something like that." Katie figured she'd wait a few more weeks before they told the children or anyone else about the baby. For now, it would be their secret. "Now off with you, through to the kitchen and I'll make breakfast."

"I've done that, *Mamm,*" James said.

"I helped," Nathan added.

James said, "Lillie is still asleep but I made breakfast for Nathan and myself. Would you like me to make some for you?"

"You'd do that?"

"*Jah,* come on. I'll show you that I can do it."

"I'm looking forward to seeing that," Katie said following the boys into the kitchen.

As she sat and watched the boys make the effort to cook the breakfast, she realized how much she'd taken for granted while being upset about Luke's death for so many years. She had been blessed with three wonderful children and she wondered if she'd truly appreciated them as much as she should have. The boys had grown up so much since Luke had died, and now Lillie was walking and talking—even giving her opinion on things.

"It's a car," James said as he rushed to the window of the kitchen. "It's Pa!"

"Already? That's strange." Katie rushed to the front door.

As soon as Mark got out of the taxi he hurried to her.

"You couldn't have finished that soon."

"The fire's still raging, but I had to come home. They can do without me for one day—on this one special day."

She pulled him into the house. "I love you, Mark."

He smiled. "I told you I'd always look after you. You're my *familye*, the four—*nee*—five of you, and you come first above all else. I'll still fight fires, but today I'm needed here with my *fraa* and *kinner*."

Mark pulled Katie into his arms and this time the last thing she cared about was getting her dress soiled.

"Pa," Lillie called out from her room.

He raised his eyebrows. "She's never acknowledged me before. This is the first time."

Katie laughed. "You should go and see what she wants."

"I'm coming, Lillie." Mark whispered into Katie's ear. "I love you too, Katie, forever and for always. Amen."

As Mark walked away to see what Lillie wanted, Katie sneaked up behind him to listen.

"What is it, Lillie?" Mark asked.

"Nothin,'" she giggled.

"Are you ready for breakfast?"

"Nee, I stay in bed."

He laughed. "You stay warm in bed, then. It's still early."

"She likes to sleep." Nathan walked past Mark to the boys' bedroom, which was beside Lillie's.

James slipped into their bedroom, too, and flung himself on his bed.

Mark turned away from Lillie's doorway and saw Katie. He gave her a smile that made her heart melt.

Katie knew she had been twice-blessed to have two great loves in one lifetime.

For I know the thoughts that I think toward you,
saith the LORD, thoughts of peace,
and not of evil, to give you an expected end.
Jeremiah 29:11

Thank you for reading The Amish Firefighter's Widow.

www.SamanthaPriceAuthor.com

THE NEXT BOOK IN THE SERIES

Book 9
Amish Widow's Secret

Cassandra never wanted to return to the Amish and follow the rules, but she soon found she was pregnant with nowhere to go.
She returned to her parents' home with the 'shameful news' only to be sent to Aunt Maud's for the remainder of her pregnancy. The other part of their plan was for Maud to find a couple who would adopt the baby. But Cassandra was never one for plans—not when they were someone else's.
Cassandra develops feelings for an Amish man at Aunt Maud's and starts to think God has a plan for her life.
But how will this young man feel about Cassandra when he learns of the secret she's been hiding?

EXPECTANT AMISH WIDOWS

Book 1 Amish Widow's Hope

Book 2 The Pregnant Amish Widow

Book 3 Amish Widow's Faith

Book 4 Their Son's Amish Baby

Book 5 Amish Widow's Proposal

Book 6 The Pregnant Amish Nanny

Book 7 A Pregnant Widow's Amish Vacation

Book 8 The Amish Firefighter's Widow

Book 9 Amish Widow's Secret

Book 10 The Middle-Aged Amish Widow

Book 11 Amish Widow's Escape

Book 12 Amish Widow's Christmas

Book 13 Amish Widow's New Hope

Book 14 Amish Widow's Story

Book 15 Amish Widow's Decision

Book 16 Amish Widow's Trust

Book 17 The Amish Potato Farmer's Widow

Book 18 Amish Widow's Tears

Book 19 Amish Widow's Heart

ALL SAMANTHA PRICE BOOK SERIES

Amish Maids Trilogy

Amish Love Blooms

Amish Misfits

The Amish Bonnet Sisters

Amish Women of Pleasant Valley

Ettie Smith Amish Mysteries

Amish Secret Widows' Society

Expectant Amish Widows

Seven Amish Bachelors

ALL SAMANTHA PRICE BOOK SERIES

Amish Foster Girls

Amish Brides

Amish Romance Secrets

Amish Twin Hearts

Amish Wedding Season

Amish Baby Collection

Gretel Koch Jewel Thief

Made in the USA
Monee, IL
24 October 2023